f a k i n g

Also by James King

The Life of Margaret Laurence
Telling Lives or Telling Lies?: Biography and Fiction
Virginia Woolf
William Blake: His Life
The Last Modern: A Life of Herbert Read
Interior Landscapes: A Life of Paul Nash
William Cowper: A Biography

Co-editor

The Letter and Prose Writings of William Cowper
William Cowper: Selected Letters

j a m e s   k i n g

f a k i n g

a novel

SIMON & PIERRE
A MEMBER OF THE DUNDURN GROUP
TORONTO · OXFORD

Editor: Marc Côté
Copyeditor: Barry Jowett
Printer: Transcontinental Printing Inc.

Canadian Cataloguing in Publication Data
King, James, 1942-
Faking

ISBN 0-88924-285-2
1. Wainewright, Thomas Griffiths, 1794-1847— Fiction. I. Title.

PS8571.I52837F34 1999   C813'.54   C99-930511-5
PR9199.3.K56F34 1999

1   2   3   4   5   03   02   01   00   99

THE CANADA COUNCIL | LE CONSEIL DES ARTS
FOR THE ARTS | DU CANADA
SINCE 1957 | DEPUIS 1957

We acknowledge the support of the **Canada Council for the Arts** for our publishing program. We also acknowledge the support of the **Ontario Arts Council** and the **Book Publishing Industry Development Program** of the **Department of Canadian Heritage.**

Printed and bound in Canada.

Printed on recycled paper.

Set in Goudy
Designed by Scott Reid

Simon & Pierre	Simon & Pierre	Simon & Pierre
8 Market Street	73 Lime Walk	2250 Military Road
Suite 200	Headington, Oxford,	Tonawanda NY
Toronto, Canada	England	U.S.A. 14150
M5E 1M6	OX3 7AD	

For my son, Alex

Look in his glommed face, his sprighte there scanne;
How woe-be-gone, how withered, forwynd, deade!

Thomas Chatterton
An Excelente Balade of Charitie,
As wroten bie the gode Prieste Thomas Rowley, 1464.

preface

I am Catherine Blake, née Haze. From a comparatively early age, I have been blessed — some would say, cursed — by the ability to communicate with the spirit world. I hear voices. As you can imagine, one cannot learn or even cultivate such a talent. I discovered my power — my only claim to distinction of any kind — as a young teenager. Two young boys — identical twins — who had drowned three months before in the river a mile or so from my family home told me of their happy existences as spirits. When, somewhat reluctantly, I got in touch with their parents, they were at first understandably sceptical of my truthfulness but, ultimately, they rejoiced at the tidings I conveyed to them. What convinced them of my veracity was the simple fact that the boys told me things — for example, their partiality to Charles Kingsley's *The Water-Babies* — only their parents could know, information which had never appeared on television or in the newspapers.

My parents were troubled by my visitations. They wanted me to be normal. The cold-war America I grew up in in the Fifties and Sixties was comfortably middle-class — like everyone else, I loved Lucy; the silver screen romances of Doris Day and Rock Hudson enthralled me. I may have been bookish, but I adored "Father Knows Best." I was one of the hordes of young women transfixed by Clint Walker's huge, magnificent chest amply displayed each week on "Cheyenne." I did draw a line, however. Poodle skirts, tight sweaters for girls, even tighter jeans for their boyfriends — principal preoccupations of young women of my generation — did not interest me. My parents, already worried that I was a social misfit, did not want me to be perceived as "touched." They forbad me to speak of what they called the "hauntings."

My parents, who worked as custodians at Cornell University at Ithaca in upper-state New York, were thrilled when the graduate student, Stephen Blake, who boarded at our ramshackle white-frame house on Lawn Street, began to court me. In those days, my blond hair — the colour of sun-ripened wheat — and the many curves nature bestowed upon my body had begun to arouse a great deal of interest on the part of the male species. In general, mother and father liked Canadians and had no objection to their only child marrying one, particularly a young professional. I suppose they were glad to be rid of the responsibility of looking after an eccentric daughter.

So, at the age of twenty, I left Ithaca for Toronto, where my husband joined the Department of Comparative Literature at the University. We have been here many years and Stephen has risen to the eminence of John Shade Professor.

My life has been a constrained one, I suppose. Although I am not one to stand on ceremony, I am Catherine, never Cathy. If I did not hear the voices, I would be considered utterly commonplace. Early on, Stephen, who is five years older and a bit of a slave to convention, decided I was not to have children. Since he has always found it difficult to accept my gift, he feared bringing into existence a brood of children who might be similarly inclined.

I have never sought employment, and I keep pretty much to myself at our large, comfortable, childless home on Admiral Road in the Annex. I shop, I cook, I read, I watch educational television. I am my husband's helpmeet.

Despite my husband's disdain for the spirit world, he was extremely pleased when — about two years after we moved into our present home — a voice told me to remodel the dining room. After I had removed about ten layers of wallpaper, I came upon a cache of money beneath the plaster and lathing. The sum of money was considerable — $42,000. Stephen decided not to report the matter to the police — we simply paid off our mortgage. A few years later, we learned that our home had once been owned by an embezzler who had stolen money from a series of gullible women. According to the account I read, the missing proceeds from his dishonesty amounted to about $45,000.

Now in my fifties, I am what the Victorians termed "a woman of noble plainness." I am also a person of a subdued temperament. Years ago, I would have been called phlegmatic. Quite recently, a friend informed me — she meant the observation kindly — I had a Prozac personality. She may have meant to say "prosaic." I am not an unintelligent person, but I must say my head spins when Stephen tells me of the various theories of literature which have infiltrated the academy. I read Anita Brookner, but I adore Maeve Binchy.

My unexceptional existence was transformed two years ago when, over a period of nine months, I received the most remarkable visitation of voices I have been privileged to witness. Up to that time, I had never heard of Thomas Wainewright, much less read a book by or about him. Also, I have never been to Australia and yet one of the documents dictated to me — the one with which this book begins — is in the unpublished archival records at the National Research Library at Canberra.

Some of the experts are still sceptical of these extraordinary communications. I have endured many slurs. I have been called a liar and labelled a fake, a writer of fiction rather than non-fiction. Tom, Eliza, Helen, Griffiths, and all the other spirits — it has been asserted — are simply projections, aspects of my personality with which I am uncomfortable. One insidious person has even insinuated that I have, in a deluded fashion, modelled myself on my namesake, the wife of the poet-illustrator. Like her famous husband, Catherine Blake witnessed visions. My accuser forgets that my husband is an academic with absolutely no interest in the denizens of the spirit world.

In light of the controversy that has made the front page of *The New York Times* and received extensive coverage in both *Newsweek* and *Time*, I have decided to make the voices available to the public, who must decide for themselves the authenticity of this "automatic" writing. Although I have been sparing in this regard, I have, when necessity demands, occasionally provided notes to assist the reader in understanding the troubled voices who have vouchsafed to entrust their memories to me. With due modesty, I trust I shall be deemed a diligent recorder and editor.

prologue

Extracts from the day records of David Carstairs (1822–1876), physician at St. Mary's Hospital, Hobart Town, Van Diemen's Land (MS 3768: Australian National Library, Canberra)

10 August 1847

Early this morning the sun was a bright lemon colour, the ocean a pale blue. But by noon the sun had become an agitated orange, the water a listless green. And, as usual, the air was so thinned that there did not seem to be any to inhale. Visited Mr. Wainewright in his room. As usual, tetchy. As I wrote down the long list of complaints he enumerated in painstaking detail, he reminded me that his surname was spelled with an "e" after the "n". I assured him I was perfectly aware of this. Many of the law reporters in England had been ignorant, he reminded me, of this crucial fact — and how could he be assured a Tasmanian physician would remember it?

His head is exceedingly long and sallow. His eyes retreat into the back of his skull, where they have an almond shape of a pronounced Oriental persuasion. His moustache drops down sadly, almost completely covering the thin tight lips. He has a harsh sibilant lisp, which causes him to bathe his immediate surroundings with a fine mist. Almost as distracting are his elongated, orange-coloured teeth, the discolouration originating in the use of tobacco. The most distinguishing characteristic of this strange face are the fine, thin lines etched vertically and horizontally in every conceivable direction.

The ferocity of his visage is undercut by Mr. Wainewright's small height and curvature of the spine. In earlier days, he would have been scarcely five foot, five inches tall. These days, he is so bowed over that he does not even reach five foot. Mr. Wainewright, who has scarcely completed his mid-forties, would easily pass for seventy.

"There is no air to breathe," he reminds me yet again. I tell him that I too cannot find any degree of comfort in the atmosphere. He feels that he is being suffocated. I have heard these complaints for many months. He wants me to provide oblivion, a bit of chloral to make him less aware of his miserable existence.

11 August 1847

Philip Jackson was closeted with Mr. Wainewright when I presented myself this afternoon. The postmaster is a large, friendly sort, whose appearance would ordinarily not cause much notice. He is bluff, big-boned, and square-jawed; his mane of carrot-red hair is his only distinguishing characteristic. Now that he is nearing fifty, the red has been invaded by the occasional coarse bristle of white. He carries, I have had to remind him many times, too much weight.

Mr. Jackson is not a person whose appearance sticks in the mind. When I saw the painter and the postmaster together this afternoon, I was reminded of Mr. Wainewright's portrait of Mr. Jackson, which the subject has somewhat ostentatiously placed above the fireplace in his sitting room. In that oil, the postmaster is a slim, refined creature possessed of a long delicate face set off with an aquiline nose, small grey eyes, and brown hair with just the faintest hint of auburn. What is even stranger is that the portrait was done from life only a year ago. Mr. Jackson thinks it a *vrai representation* of himself and sings its praises continuously. Never have I seen a portrait which bore so little resemblance to the life it is supposed to represent. I have been careful to say nothing in town of this, but surely others have noticed the bizarre discrepancy?

13 August 1847

The air is sucked dry of the tiniest bit of moisture. Surprisingly, Mr. Wainewright did not have any grievances today. He reminisced about his early days in the penal colony, in particular of the stench when amputated arms and legs were consigned to the fire at the nearby Colonial Hospital, where he was first employed. He even discoursed at length on the various limbs he had seen floating in the stream near the hospital. He also discoursed on my one of my predecessors, Dr. Brodribb, whom he once assisted. The poor man died during an outbreak of typhoid, the physician unable to cure himself.

14 August 1847

I gather that his fellow prisoners detest Mr. Wainewright, not so much because his portrait painting has allowed him an *entrée* into the reception rooms and salons of Hobart Town but because he has the reputation of transmitting any information he can gather on them to the authorities. Although he has denied these allegations, Mr. Wainewright is very much in isolated confinement — perhaps of his own devising.

Mr. Wainewright, who envisions me a comrade of sorts, has told me at great length of the magnificent landscape of Sydney Harbour which has been assigned to him by some local collector. Mr. Wainewright chuckled: "I never saw the port of Sydney, much less painted it."

15 August 1847

Today's discourse is on the Conditional Pardon granted to him in December 1845. "I am no longer a prisoner. I am supposedly here of my own free will. I can travel anywhere in the Australian states, but the irony is that I am now far too weak to go anywhere. My broken spine traps me here."

16 August 1847

Mr. Wainewright may be dying. He has suffered a paralysis of the right side and is without speech. All the colour has vanished from his countenance, as if he had seen a ghost. His eyes are opened wide. Spoke yet again of the dream that occurs over and over: "the sweetest little boy I ever saw" dances up to his bedside. "He seemed just out of leading strings, yet I took particular notice of the firmness and steadiness of his tread." At first, the apparition apparently "harmonized" his spirits, but now he thinks it promises him a comfort that will always be denied him.

I asked if the child looked like his own son, but he dismissed this possibility as an irrelevance: "My dreams have either tinged my mind with melancholy or filled it with terror, and the effect has been unavoidable. If we swallow arsenic, we must be poison'd, and he who dreams as I have done must be troubled."

17 August 1847
The patient died during the night. He did not speak again, but he tried to move his body in a sort of rocking motion, as if he were trying to escape from the pitiful shell in which he had long been a prisoner.

Tom

I

First things first. Let's begin with the basic story
of my wretched existence. More accurately, the
grid that has been imposed on it:

Chambers Biographical Dictionary
(Revised Edition, 1986), p. 1387.

WAINEWRIGHT, Thomas Griffiths
(1794–1847), English art critic, painter,
forger, and probably poisoner, was born
at Chiswick. He took to writing (as
"Janus Weathercock", &c.) art
criticisms and miscellaneous articles for
the periodicals. He married, and, soon
outrunning his means, committed
forgery (1822, 1824), and almost
certainly poisoned with strychnine his

half sister-in-law (1830), probably also his uncle
(1828), mother-in-law (1830) and possibly others.
The sister-in-law had been fraudulently insured for
£12,000, but actions to enforce payment failed; and
Wainewright, venturing back from France in 1837,
was sentenced to life transportation for his old
forgery. In Van Diemen's Land (Tasmania) he
painted portraits, ate opium and died in Hobart
hospital. He is the "Varney" of Lytton's *Lucretia*
(1846) and the "Slinkton" of Dickens' *Hunted Down*
(1860). See his *Essays and Criticisms*, edited, with a
memoir, by W.C. Hazlitt (1880); B.W. Procter's
Autobiography (1877), Oscar Wilde's *Intentions*
(1891), J. Curling, *Janus Weathercock* (1938), and R.
Crossland, *Wainewright in Tasmania* (1954).

There I am — a bee in amber — reduced to a capsule
biography filled with half-truths and lies. My life has served
as a "model" for the imaginations of Bulwer-Lytton and
Dickens. I should be honoured? I suffered infamy and have
been rewarded by being immortalized in a fifth-rate work by
Dickens and by a third-rate novelist? In me, Oscar Wilde
(Wilde?!) discerned a diseased imagination.

Motivation is usually hard to discover in biographical
dictionaries; only so-called facts or events are there.
However, I see a slight glimmer of hope in *Chambers'* use of
"probably" and "almost certainly" in my entry. If there is
room for some doubt, I shall take that opportunity.

We think we know, but we know very little. How
many of you have wandered through the Tate and paused
before Henry Wallis' *Death of Thomas Chatterton*? The
long torso of the recently deceased forger languidly
propels itself from a dishevelled bed towards the spectator.
The mane of ginger hair is swept back to reveal a delicate,
slightly upturned nose, high cheek bones, perfectly arched
eyebrows, excessively refined (almost effeminate) mouth
and eyes. This is the famous forger and poet reduced to
penury. He has just destroyed all his papers (incriminating

evidence), and, at last, he has surrendered himself to peaceful death.

This painting has become the icon of the isolated artist, cast asunder by a cruel, heedless world. Remember though, the portrait of Chatterton is pure invention on Wallis' part, for no likeness survived the poor youth's death in 1770. The poet and novelist George Meredith posed for that painting; in fact, that canvas is a monument in more ways than one to the hazards of the artistic life: Wallis ran away with Meredith's wife.

You *were* quite certain what Tom Chatterton looked like. You *think* you know the essential truths of Tom Wainewright.

When I had a body to call my own, two settings predominated, although I have never had the luxury of a real home. First, picture the sitting room at Linden House, my grandfather's residence, in the 1810s, where I supplanted Augustan austerity in favour of Regency elegance. An enormous Turkey carpet, in which are embedded garlands of warm pink, crimson red, lavender purple flowers. The green leaves are almost black, so that the flowers leap out as you cross the floor. An *original* cast of the Venus de Medici, with ivory white eyes, pointed breasts, and chastely veiled *mons*. My companions. Neptune, a large, coal-black Newfoundland. Julia, a tortoiseshell beloved of the dog. He is insufferably friendly, she has to be tamed by gentle usage. Further touches. A few hot-house plants on a grey marble slab. A Fuseli painting, in which lovers melt into each other. All of the above bathed in a Caravaggio kind of light, breathed through the painted glass of the lamp. I am truly at home reclining by a winter fireside in my pomona-green *chaise-lounge*, a full glass of Vino d'Este in my left hand while my right strokes puss to a full and sonorous purr.

That room vanishes. Now, I see another chamber. This dank and rat-infested hell-hole is of the Tasmanian mode. The air is so heavy that one struggles to breathe, as if in the

19

grips of two huge lobster pincers squeezing one's lungs, tearing them asunder. As if a malicious giant had pressed his thumbs against the base of my little chicken bone of a neck.

What brought me — a true exquisite — to Tasmania in 1837? This is a snippet from Official History, an entry in the Record Book of Colonial Offences: "*Transported on ship 'Susan' 21 November 1837. Life. Married 1 Child. Stated that his offence was : 'Forging a power of Attorney in order to come into possession of my own monies. Wife Eliza. I have been separated from her for some years.'*"

It's strange how I or the stenographer took so much trouble about my son and wife. But Eliza and I were nothing to each other. *Because* we were nothing to each other everything that made me so famous and so unhappy came about. And I wasn't really transported to Hobart in Van Diemen's (No Man's) Land because of forgery. I was transported because I was an artist who had lost his way. *Because* I supposedly had the misfortune to be loved by Helen Abercromby. *Because* — it is alleged — I murdered her. In love and sometimes in war, everything is fair. But what about the man who tries to play by the rules that govern his life? who tries his best with the shabby hand of cards dealt him?

According to some of my detractors, I had no character. Or not enough. They simply besmirched that which I had none of or not enough of.

E.g. John Camden Hotten. Publisher.
1845. Hotten: "*Why did you poison your sister-in-law?*"
Wainewright: "*Why, I don't know, except that she had such thick ankles.*"
Twenty-one years later, he changed his story:
1866. Hotten: "*At another time some one asked him how he could have been so heartless as to murder a loving, trusting young girl like*"

Miss Phoebe Abercromby. 'I scarcely know myself,' replied he, with a yawn and a sneer, 'unless it was that her legs were too thick.'"

What rot! It was Hotten who did not know the difference between ankles and legs. My "supposed" beloved was named Madeleine (Phoebe was her *third* name). In 1845, I answered a question; twenty years later, he claims, I yawned and sneered. Ankles or legs, my roguish reply to Hotten has been taken as if I was *seriously* replying to his question.

Is Hotten's testimony reliable? Should I be convicted of murder because of a sly rejoinder? Does facetiousness make one a murderer? Since I want you to take a real interest in me, I guess I'll have to submit to a further imposition, a physical. I'll tell you about most of my organs, although I hope you'll permit me a modicum of privacy. In vermin-infested Van Diemen's Land, a prison description is, appropriately enough, a "mugging." On 22 November 1837, the day I became 2325, the following measurements were made: "Name: Wainewright Griffiths Thomas; Trade: Painter; Height (without shoes): 5/5 1/2; Age: 43; Complexion: Pale; Head: Oval; Hair: Brown; Whiskers: Ditto; Forehead: High; Eyebrows: Brown; Eyes: Grey; Nose: Long; Mouth: Large; Chin: Long; Remarks: None."

Who decides that eyes are grey instead of blue, that a mouth is "large," that there should be NO "remarks"?

Today, I have some remarks. John Forster, who visited me in Newgate, claimed my hair was sandy; Hazlitt said it was dark; in *Lucretia* — a novel based in large part on my life, the hero has yellow tresses. Julian Ellis said: "His hair was sandy, but he dyed it black." The Contessa di Guiccioli, Mrs. Leigh Hunt, and Sheldrake said Byron's club foot was on the left; Hobhouse and Thomas Moore maintained it was on the right. The colour of my hair has become as controversial as the whereabouts of that maniac poet's club foot.

21

Hazlitt said I stooped slightly whereas Talfourd maintained that I carried myself with a military bearing. Was I dumpy and commonplace (as one wag suggested) or was I a glamorous man about town (the majority opinion)?

Back to that simple-minded list and its short, dull answers. Under "Remarks," why not mention the disseminated sclerosis that hastened my death? Why not refer to my "fidgety nervous manner," a trait mentioned by all the many biographers who have turned their snouts in my direction? If I was such a villain, why is "painter" the only distinguishing characteristic in the mugging?

I have many, many questions about my own life. Far more than the self-serving likes of Dickens or Bulwer-Lytton ever asked. For the moment, I shall not glance at the biographers who have written such drivel about me, although I am galled to see that in Peter Ackroyd's endless pages on Dickens I am awarded the briefest of mentions — I deserve at least half a page.

I have obviously returned to set the record straight. From whence have I come? Where dwells my raging, unbounded spirit? One commentator had the decency to admit he was stumped: "As it is, we know nothing. The end, as the beginning, is cast in shadow. We have now, it is true, and for the first time, the official record of Wainewright's death. But we still do not know where he was buried; whether, indeed, he was decently buried at all. Perhaps his worn-out body found its way to a cold slab in the dissecting room; perhaps his fugitive biographers were not truly in error, after all, and the end finally was 'under circumstances too painful to be recapitulated.' We can only guess."

My spirit has never been put to rest, subject as it has been to countless aspersions. In any event, I shall tell the truth, my truth being much more interesting than that in the reams of paper and gallons of ink that the writers of so-called non-fiction have bestowed on me. Those cannibals, ever on the prey for a corpse on which to feast, have created the most amazing fictions. Now, I have nothing to lose and, since I am dead, nothing to gain. Who can better tell the truth than such a fugitive autobiographer?

II

Why am I now reduced to a harum-scarum kind of writing, a maker of lists? I bet you are discomfited. You are saying to yourself: this fellow darts from thing to thing. He does not tell a tale with a beginning, a middle, and an end. Moreover, his language has lost the accent of the nineteenth century. There are new laws of mimesis, and I have always been a person to anticipate fashion, not merely drag along in its wake.*

So, I *shouldn't* have to tell you in painstaking detail of my miserable childhood, but I shall. My mother died giving birth to me. I supposed I killed her. Then my father vanished. I was an orphan. I felt lonely and guilty. My grandfather — my guardian — despised me. My uncle could not make up his mind about me. Was I a little murderer? Or was I one of Fortune's many victims? I suffered cruelly. What else is really new? Maybe nothing much, but every man plays his own variation on the melody of loss and despair.

Orphans never have choices. The greatest cruelty they sometimes endure is the illusion of choice. Particularly cruel is to give them any kind of possible hope that they have misread the landscape of their desolation. At Linden House in Turnham Green, my grandfather's home, I was made to breathe the air of sufferance. This tiny hamlet in the northern portion of Chiswick had been the haunt of highwaymen in previous centuries, no traveller safe who used its roads. When I lived there, bodily danger had given way — for me — to the spiritual kind.

---

*EDITOR'S NOTE: My husband — although he is a literary historian and most certainly not a literary theorist — has informed me that Tom's "discourse" is post-modern, is filled with what are called erasures, aporias, and gaps, and has been unduly influenced by the unholy trinity of Derrida, Lacan, and Barthes.

In its way, the house was a tribute to the previous century. Every element was pristine, balanced, and, above all, elegant. The rooms were large, without ostentation, each piece of furniture announcing itself with quiet majesty; although spacious and wide, the corridors unfortunately bestowed upon the building the feel of a public institution. "I am the creation of a man of considerable taste," Linden House whispered. A house of too much balance, a critic of a different persuasion might have proclaimed. For me, it had a sepulchre-like feel. Never enough life, not enough intimacy. Certainly not a house in which any youngster would have felt at liberty to wander. I was never allowed into the sitting room with its sofas upholstered in silk of the faintest pink; I was not welcome in the dining room because I might open the doors of the breakfront and perhaps break a ginger jar; I was not to place myself in the entrance hall in case a visitor mistook me for one of the help.

The servants were kindly disposed towards me, particularly little Miss Walsh, the housekeeper, who had crossed over to England from Ireland as a young child. A thin string of a woman with electric shocks of red hair, Sarah found it difficult to control her feelings about her dead parents. Whenever she mentioned them, her ivory-coloured face would turn a bright pink, at one with her tresses. Placed in service at the age of eight, she had never really overcome her love for those who had sold her away.

Touching forty when I knew her, she loved the grounds of Linden House, often exclaiming how "Irish" they were. (We all make idiosyncratic adjustments to life's deprivations.) Tiny rivulets ran in and out of huge moss-coloured stones at the edge of the estate. The various kinds of beech which comprised the little interior forest of the grounds were an additional source of pleasure. The Druidic side of her nature was aroused by the hillocks confined within the trees. There, the ground looked almost pregnant, as if some sort of creature waited to emerge. As I climbed them, I would come across little pieces of cornices and other kinds of rubble. Some sort of ruin, completely victimized by nature's cunning acquisitiveness, was hidden from our eyes. Miss Walsh thought it was some sort of miniature Stonehenge whereas even then I knew the chunks of stone were Roman.

Above all, her joy was resolutely centred on the huge pond which fronted the forest. In spring, we would walk round it, while she discoursed on the wild flowers which hugged its edges, talking almost non-stop about their idiosyncrasies.

One day, she abruptly interrupted one of her musings. "Child, you are about to turn six. What will you do with your life? Will you be a man of letters like your grandfather?"

Even then, I thought it a strange question. "I don't know. I have been told I have exceedingly limited prospects."

"I don't think that can be so. Mr. Griffiths has high expectations of you."

"On the contrary, he has told me I must not entertain any such notions. I must be careful not to get above myself. Those were his very words."

Her face became violently red, her hands fluttering. "I am sure you are mistaken. My parents often seemed harsh, but I know they wanted the best for me. You are seeing merely one side of the Master's countenance."

I did not bother to respond, but I must admit that I began to wonder if she was correct, if my grandfather's coldness had a complementary gentle side. Was he Janus-like? and had I failed to see this? A semblance of hope gained entry into my already guarded soul.

III

"Who killed my mother?"

"Why, sirrah, it was you! In childbed."

My grandfather, some said, was a plain-spoken man. In fact, he made such a virtue into a vice. He had been born in Stone in Staffordshire and, at fourteen, apprenticed to a watchmaker. On the day in August 1802 that he made this revelation, we were strolling in the garden at Linden House.

I was five. We had been wandering aimlessly through the four acres and had just arrived outside the house. Before my grandfather spoke, I had been daydreaming, marvelling anew at the building's coy Palladian austerity. We were just about to go inside. My eyes had been darting back and forth to the two Floras who guarded the entrance, their breasts standing firm under their drapery. Then, abruptly, he turned to face me, declaring that Ann had been slaughtered. This led to my very justifiable question, which he considered an impertinence.

My grandfather's immense shadow loomed over me. As usual, he refused to look me in the eye. "My girl was a great loss." He went on, mumbling: "She understood the writings of Mr. Locke as well as, perhaps, any person, of either sex, now living."

A strange thing for a father to say? Maybe not, for Ralph was one of the most celebrated publishers of his day, a man whose magnificent home had been manufactured off the backs of countless Grub Street hacks. Today, his name still has all the tinges of bibliographic respectability firmly attached to it: founding editor of *The Monthly Review*.

He was not an intellectual, just someone who knows that there are lots of readers who enjoy seeing the writings of others carved up. The real source of Ralph's wealth was pornography. In 1750 he published *Fanny Hill, or the Memoirs of a Woman of Pleasure*. The obscure author — John Cleland, an ex-consul of Smyrna, was reprimanded by the Privy Council. A bookseller, with the appropriate surname of Drybutter, was sent to the pillory. Ralph's profit ran to ten thousand pounds. The smut-pedlar escaped recrimination and gaol — and he even inserted a puffing notice in the usually solemn *Review*: "The stile has a peculiar neatness, and the characters are naturally drawn.... As to the step lately taken to suppress this book, we really are at a loss to account for it." I like that expression "naturally drawn." It has just the right amount of understatement. Of course, later, I, like many other hot-bloods, would be "naturally drawn" to this book.

Born poor, Ralph, the ex-watchmaker, craved respectability. He had high hopes for his daughter, my poor mother Ann, who from early age demonstrated an intellect of extraordinary capability. And then she had the misfortune to become romantically attached to Tom Wainewright, a wastrel, and marry him. She ventured into even more forbidden terrain when she conceived a child and then permanently deserted her father when she lost her life giving me mine.

I was never to be forgiven. Against my will (or, more accurately, without any volition whatsoever), I took his most prized possession away from Ralph. And so — despite Miss Walsh's cock-eyed optimism — I was punished. He had no power over my rascal father, who simply vanished.

Not only did he disappear, I do not know (despite the most assiduous research on my part) which Thomas Wainewright was my father. Was he the Thomas Wainewright who appears on the Law Lists? Or, was he the man of the same name who was a chemist and a member of the Apothecaries' Company, who had a shop at 19 Pall Mall? One particularly malicious biographer has suggested that my skill as a poisoner points to the chemist as my father. Unfounded speculation based on unfounded speculation — a good example of biographers building sand castles upon shifting sand. I can only imagine my sire and dam. I suspect both were people of fashion, beautiful of face and dress. I like to think I am a worthy son to two remarkable individuals.

My grandsire vented the full force of his enmity in my direction. Surface-wise, I was given the best. My education at Greenwich Academy was resolutely classical, under the "bibliomaniac" Charles Burney, son of the great music man and brother of that infamous scribbler, Fanny.* Not much to report on my residency there. The usual British routine. I was bullied and then became a bully. I was sodomized and

*EDITOR'S NOTE: My husband has pointed out to me that this writer is now, *de rigueur*, referred to as Frances Burney (D'Arblay) by literary critical feminists. The nickname is, he tells me, extremely "problematical."

then sodomized others. Very hierarchical. You always (if you get my meaning) knew where you stood. I was a more than tolerable scholar. Not outstanding, just very good.

Perhaps the extent of Ralph's dislike of me can be discerned in his conduct at tea-time one afternoon. Except for his small, receding, raisin eyes, he was a man of coarse features. On this particular day — I must have been six — he scoured me carefully, as if on the prowl to unmask my shortcomings. A very nervous Sarah — she could read my grandfather's mind — suggested I show him the small coloured paper boxes I had assiduously manufactured. A bit startled, he held them up in his giant paw of a hand for a few seconds, inspected them by placing each in close proximity to his bulbous nose, then one by one placed them in his mouth and swallowed them. A very agitated Sarah whisked me away when I burst into tears.

My young life was traumatic but within bounds of normalcy. All of this changed when Ralph died 28 September 1803, in his eighty-third year. According to the *Annual Register*, grandfather was "a firm friend, a cordial lover of the enjoyments of domestic happiness, and a successful promoter of the charms of social intercourse." I had many reasons to challenge the bland observations of the *Register*.

I could not summon any tears for Ralph, but I was forced to mourn his money:

Will of Dr. Ralph Griffiths, June 7, 1803
Extracted from the Principal Registry of
the
Probate, Divorce, and Admiralty Division of
The High Court of Justice

This is the last Will and Testament of me, Ralph Griffiths, of Turnham Green in the County of Middlesex, Doctor of Laws. Whereas on the marriage of my late daughter Ann Griffiths with the late Thomas Wainewright, Esquire, I advanced a certain sum of money and covenanted that after my death a further sum should be paid by my personal representatives as a marriage portion for my said daughter, and whereas my grandson Thomas Wainewright is become entitled to such property so advanced by me to his mother, my will is that neither he, the said Thomas Wainewright, nor his trustees for him shall demand any further sum out of my estate as I hereby declare that the sum already paid with that which is covenanted to be paid is all that I intend for my said grandson.

My grandfather left me only that which he could not, without a great deal of difficulty, deny me: £5000 in annuities. In addition to disinheriting a helpless nine-year-old, my grandfather removed my middle name, Griffiths. Since I had taken something from Ralph, everything had to be taken from me. I was not to be allowed a life in the grand style to which I aspired.

I was a fake. I appeared to be a high-spirited, ribald boy, but I was really a murderer. For me, appearances have always been deceiving.

IV

At the age of nine, I was left in the care of my uncle, George Edward. In contrast to my grandfather, my uncle was a slight wisp of a man. Unfailingly kind and gentle, he had lived his entire life in the wake of his father's mean-spirited bumptiousness. He melted into things, never seeming to be completely in any room into which he wandered. From an early age, he had been taught that any display of personality on his part was an abomination to his father. He learned the lesson well.

Uncle was resolutely solicitous of my welfare when I was at Turnham Green during school holidays. More often than not, he referred to me affectionately as his "little man." As he got older, despite the curvature of the spine which made him into a sort of walking pretzel, his good nature still prevailed. I liked my uncle, although from early on I could sense that his politeness and many kindnesses masked a complete indifference to others. I don't think he even had much affection for himself.

I must own up. I was not a good child. I was one of those legendary, horrible boys who captures various kinds of insects in order to torture them. In the spirit of experimentation, I removed their heads and enjoyed seeing the strange, zig zag movements of a butterfly or a moth in such moments, those thrilling seconds when their bodies are surprised that no head survives to guide them into the safety of the air.

Most boys practise wanton cruelty in one way or other. Miss Walsh knew this, but she would take me roundly to task when she came upon me engaging in my hobby. Her brow riddled with twice the usual number of lines and the quaver in her voice betrayed the struggle between fury at such cruelty and pity for the orphan boy who resorted to such repulsive activities. "Come, Tom, you can find other ways to amuse yourself," she would often begin. Then, in order to distract me, would force me to accompany her on her daily promenade.

It was she, shortly before her death, who must have suggested to my uncle that he should allow me to accompany him on one of his many visits to London. My uncle demurred, but she insisted in her quiet way. Of course, she scolded him, I wouldn't be interested in his publishing activities, but she was sure my adolescent nature would be enthralled by attending one of the conjuring displays he frequented.

Uncle had published all manner of books on the various forms of magic and knew how most of the more elementary tricks were generated. His imagination — such as it was — was riveted by those practitioners who could perform feats, the methodologies of which had never been placed into print because, they claimed, they were not vulgar conjurers who practised illusion: in reality, they brazenly asserted, they possessed the power to convert material objects into thin air — or vice-versa. My uncle maintained these magicians were clever liars, but he wasn't absolutely sure. He claimed he wanted to catch them out. He lied. For him, these men were the only ministers whose creeds and rites attracted him. Fragile though such a belief system might seem, it offered my uncle the faint hope that there was some sort of spiritual dimension beyond the crudities of the material world.

The odours of the real world confronted us in the neighbourhood of Mr. Kumar, in a runt of a street which did

31

not deserve its place in the heart of Mayfair. The terraced row of houses which we beheld were not so much shabby as dissolute. Although no brickwork had fallen away, each of the ones I could see were deeply gouged and cracked, almost to the point where the mortar would no longer confine them. Repulsive odours of piss, shit, and ordure emanated from what passed for gutters. After we descended from the carriage which had brought us to the conjurer's residence, we were both overwhelmed by another foul smell, that coming from the stench of carcasses of cats and dogs being roasted in the open flames by the beggars who inhabited the nearby alleys.

Our knock was quickly answered, as if the maid were well aware that her master's clients would vanish if the door was not opened *subito*. The young woman who gave us entry was comely if swarthy, obviously a refugee from Mr. Kumar's homeland. Her costume was the proper one but slovenly showed the remains of several meals. From the small entrance way, we gained the small sitting room, fitted out with two small wooden chairs. The blinds drawn shut, an absence of pictures on the walls painted a ghastly shade of mauve, and the fifty or so votive candles that filled most of the floor space gave the room just the correct unworldly atmosphere. Mr. Kumar would not be long, she assured us as she dashed from the room, closing the door behind her.

My uncle confided to me that he had heard truly amazing things of Mr. Kumar's gifts. Evidently, he performed only at home and only to small assemblages, under no circumstances to exceed five. We had to wait only a short time for the door to be opened again, this time by a damsel clad in harem finery. Through the pale blue cotton in which she was decked one could see large, beautifully shaped breasts and, lower down, a shock of black pudendal hair. I was sure it was the same woman who had shown us into the house. This time, she spoke no words. She bowed, nudging us in the direction of the adjoining room.

When my uncle pushed open that door, we were

confronted by a brightly lit, windowless room. Except for the illumination, the room had absolutely no furnishings. Not a large room, its bareness bestowed a slight echo. We stood there for a few moments before Mr. Kumar joined us. A tall, dark person of many sharp angles, he was clad in a shirt and trousers made from what looked like black linen. He wore nothing else: no jewellery, no shoes, and, much to my disappointment, no turban. He greeted both of us warmly, bending down to take my hand. When he spoke, he swooped the air with his arms and hands. Assuring us it was a great honour to receive persons of our distinction, he proceeded directly to business.

"My skills are exceedingly limited. I have been given," he pointed a bit ostentatiously to his temple, "the power to enact only a few visions of the transcendent reality that controls our universe." Pausing for emphasis, he continued: "I have been loathe to appear in any kind of theatre or circus to display my capabilities because I would then consort with those who do not care to understand the implications of what you are about to see." I think this was by way of explaining why my uncle had agreed to pay him fifty guineas. Mr. Kumar's "Mysterious East" was obviously a refined commodity, not available to riffraff.

He then assured us that the best displays of the energy of the universe were simple and best performed in a way which allowed the witnesses to be completely sure of the "veracity" of what they beheld. He clapped his hands and Salomé — as her employer called her — entered the room, this time holding before her a large bamboo cage containing approximately ten canaries. Undisturbed by our presence, the birds sang, their beautiful trills taking on a deep vibrato in the furniture-less room. Mr. Kumar asked me to approach the cage, opened its door and encouraged me to allow a few of the inhabitants to settle on my hand. Several did so promptly, seeming to take pleasure in my company. These birds were extraordinarily tame. Deeply trusting of human contact, they craved affection in an almost canine manner. I was both touched and captivated.

33

The fakir — I have never been one to resist a pun — then informed us that he would be performing a simple "visionary experience" for us, one in which as witnesses we had to be exactly seven feet away from him. Salomé handed the cage to her master, left the room, and returned immediately with a pole and a large white piece of cotton. She approached my uncle with this cloth. Mr. Kumar asked him to examine it carefully. He did so and returned it to her. Then, the magician asked my uncle to prod the ceiling and all four walls with the pole. He also requested that he inspect the integrity of the floor. I suppose we were being assured that there were no hidden fissures or trap doors. My uncle pronounced himself satisfied. Salomé then placed the pole in a corner and proceeded to cover the cage with the cloth. She wrapped it loosely but carefully and then retired to the corner where she had placed the pole.

Mr. Kumar spoke to us of the special powers which the "benign providence of the universe had vouchsafed" to give him. His speech began to take on a laboured, guttural quality, sweat now pouring profusely down his face. Slowly, he raised the cloth-entrapped cage, muttering a gibberish assortment of phrases and expressions. Suddenly, he stopped. Then, he shrieked, the way one might spit out a stream of obscenities. Salomé rushed up to him and tugged away at the cloth, which fell to the ground. The cage and its inmates had vanished into thin air.

My uncle was both startled and amazed, strange emotions for him. As for me, a profusion of tears overwhelmed me. My three companions rushed over, assuring me no harm would befall me. I cared nothing for their assurances because once again I felt cheated. The feeling was simple enough: the birds had enthralled me and then been violently removed. Those were the reflections which made me sob uncontrollably. Mr. Kumar offered me the assurance that all birds are creatures of the air and live eternally in that element, whether we can see them or not. Salomé had the goodness to seem ashamed of having given me a fright. My uncle was embarrassed by my wanton display of emotion, but he said nothing. He must have wondered what kind of ingrate I was to react hysterically to what was supposed to have been a pleasant outing.

Shortly after we arrived back at Linden House, Sarah became suddenly and violently ill, coughing up blood. The next day she was confined to her tiny excuse for a bedchamber. A week later, she passed away. I visited her only once during her final agony. Taking no notice of her own condition, she wanted to speak about my future.

"You must be a good lad. Listen attentively to your uncle. He is a creature of great virtue." Then, she looked me in the eye: "You are a child of wondrous talent. Someday, you will be reunited with your dear mama."

I nodded my head in compliance.

This seemed to give her considerable satisfaction. "I am about to be reunited with my parents. The day of my death will be my happiest." These declarations were uttered with considerable warmth. I nodded once again. She placed her two frail little hands together, as if in prayer. "Visit me tomorrow."

She died during the night. I am not ashamed to confess I shed copious tears. After all, she was the only person I had ever known who showed me any warmth. My uncle's kindness was tantalizing, but it never amounted to anything. He was not unduly bothered when, at the age of eighteen, I announced my intent to depart Linden House and make my way in the world. He smiled wanly when I broached the subject and presented me with ten gold sovereigns on the day I left his care.

No *real* profession appealed to me. Since I had no religious beliefs, I would have made an excellent cleric. But that life was too sedentary for someone as easily distracted as myself. I was too much of a would-be spendthrift (although I had no experience in that line at the time) to go into commerce. I drifted.

The little attention I could give to anything was directed to painting, or rather the admiration of it. I had even then more than a modicum of taste. I had also started to show what is now called "attitude." I was opinionated. I spoke hastily, directly, and with gusto. I was not shy of visiting disdain on all manner of things. If someone asked my thoughts on a piece of verse or a canvas that did not meet my standards, I was not politic in giving vent to my choler.

What I began to notice was that my hand — with virtually no training — could replicate exactly what my eye beheld. I was never troubled with originality — I was merely an excellent copyist. So I decided to specialize in the human face.

At nineteen, I entered the portrait studio of Thomas Phillips, a large rambling man, in Hanover Square. Phillips, who had begun as a glass-painter in Birmingham, was sometimes not inclined to take his famous sitters too seriously. Once, bursting often into wheezing guffaws, he told me how he had teased Mr. Blake mercilessly about his supposed communication with the archangel Gabriel: "Evil spirits love to assume the looks of good ones; and this may have been done to mislead you." Blake, who was quite capable of scepticism, had asked the angel for proof of his pedigree. The angel promised him "good assurance," whereupon Blake became aware of a shining shape with bright wings. This creature waved his hands, whereupon the roof of Blake's study opened, the spirit ascended into heaven, stood in the sun, and moved the universe. "An angel or a devil could not have done that — it was the archangel Gabriel." Mr. Phillips winked at me to express his disdain for the "proof" offered him by his sitter.

My employment at Phillips was to size canvases. In addition, I was occasionally allowed to add an inconsequential hill or mountain top to the extreme right or left of the upper background of the portrait of some knight of the glen. Or, I touched up the decorations on the costumes of Dowager Countesses. Constantly, Phillips exhorted me to attend to detail. He did not fancy himself an artist — he was producing high-quality products at outlandish prices to the seriously rich, who could be incredibly fussy.

In this way, I remained a humble witness to the lives of the great. In these reduced circumstances, I encountered the insufferable Coleridge who corrected my German and the pedantical laureate Robert Southey. Although Phillips was no Gainsborough or Romney, he was not a hack. I learned a great deal from him. I could have become a good, if not great, portrait painter.

Then Phillips was graced with the most renowned sitter of his career: George Gordon, Lord Byron. He sat to Phillips for two portraits, one of them in Albanian costume. In that astounding outfit — the turban of salmon pink and forest green, the splendid tribal coat of red embroidered lavishly with gold — the man is transformed into his persona: Childe Harold, the extravagant, aristocratic, world-weary Englishman doomed to roam the East for an answer to the meaning of life. In a letter to his mother, Byron boasted of his acquisition of some magnificent Albanian dresses, "the only expensive articles in this country, they cost 50 guineas each." In that same letter, he mentions his acquaintance with two ten-year-old boys: "They are totally unlike our lads, have painted complexions like rouged dowagers, large black eyes & features perfectly regular. They are the prettiest little animals I ever saw."

Whilst the great man was in the studio, I would steal into a narrow corner and sketch him. His countenance was a marvel: ivory skin providing the perfect contrast for his perfectly chiselled eyes and nose. Here was the English Adonis, although the dimple, the thin moustache, and the feminine inclination of the mouth provided a subtle contrast to his otherwise aggressive masculinity. He had begun to go to fat, but my employer wisely kept any hint of that tendency out of his rendition. Phillips never noticed my presence, but one day I saw a gleam in Byron's eye as he caught sight of me in the shadows.

As he was leaving the studio that day, Byron accosted me. He reminded me that John Murray had commissioned

Phillips and not an insignificant little apprentice to paint his portrait. But perhaps, after all, I could make myself useful. He directed me to meet him that evening at a house on magnificent Albemarle Street, then *the* watering-hole of those denizens of society who are on show to the world.

Should I perhaps draw a veil over the sordid events of the following week at that bordello? Should it suffice to say that I performed many services for Lord Byron? That the great poet frequently knelt before me? I could tell you to use your imagination, but, as it happens, one eyewitness to our activities penned her observations, which subsequently saw their way into print. This enterprising whore, who had previously serviced Byron, applied her eye to a peephole which gave her command of the cubicle to which Byron and I had been assigned:

> *The eldest might be, on my nearest guess, towards twenty-five, a tall comely young man, in a white fustian frock, with a green velvet cap.*
>
> *The youngest could not be above seventeen, fair, ruddy, compleatly well made, and to say the truth, a sweet pretty stripling.*
>
> *But after a look of circumspection which I saw the eldest cast every way round the room, probably in too much hurry and heat not to overlook the very small opening I was posted at, especially at the height it was, whilst my eye too close to it, kept the light from shining through, and betraying it; he said something to his companion that presently chang'd the face of things.*
>
> *For now the elder began to embrace, to press, to kiss the younger, to put his hands in his bosom, and give manifest signs of an amorous intention. In the rashness then of their young ages, and bent as they were to accomplish their project of preposterous pleasure, at the risque of the very worse consequences, where a discovery was nothing less than improbable, they now proceeded to such lengths as soon satisfied me what they were.*

For presently the eldest unbutton'd the other's breeches, and removing the linen barrier, brought out to view a plump white shaft, an engine of prodigious size, when after handling, and playing with and sucking it, with other dalliance, all receiv'd by the boy with some opposition, he got him to turn round with his face from him, to a chair that stood hard by, when knowing, I suppose, his office, the Ganymede now obsequiously lean'd his head against the back of it, and projecting his body, made a fair mark, still cover'd with his shirt, as he thus stood in a side-view to meet but fronting his companion, who presently unmasked his battery of the middle-size.

Slipping then aside the young lad's shirt, and tucking it up under his cloaths behind, he shew'd to the open air, those globular, fleshy eminences that compose the mount-pleasants of Rome, and which now, with all the narrow vale that intersects them, stood display'd, and expos'd to his attack: nor could I without a shudder, behold the dispositions he made for it. First then, moistening well with spittle his instrument, obviously to render it glib, he pointed, he introduc'd it, as I could plainly discern, not only from its direction, and my losing sight of it; but by the writhing, twisting, and soft murmur'd complaints of the young sufferer; but, at length, the first straights of entrance being pretty well got through, every thing seem'd to move, and go pretty currently on, as in a carpet-road, without much rub, or resistance: and now passing one hand round his minion's hips, he got hold of his enormous red-topt ivory toy, that stood perfectly stiff, and showed, that if he was like his mother behind he was like his father before; this the older man diverted himself with, whilst with the other hand, he wanton'd with his lover's hair, and leaning forward over his back, drew his face, from which the boy shook the loose curls that fell over it, in the posture he stood him in, and brought him towards his, so as to receive a long-breathe'd kiss, after which,

renewing his driving, and thus continuing to harass his
rear, the height of the fit came on with its usual
symptoms.

As you can appreciate, I had soon tired of this older,
twenty-six-year-old man, who had the propensity to
discourse endlessly on his melancholia. Or to spend hours
talking of the poetry of the hunchback, Alexander Pope,
whose description of the sylphs in *The Rape of the Lock* —
"the Light militia of the air" — he considered nothing short
of divine.* Besides, I did not share Byron's form of "natural"
inclinations. When I made my disdain known, the poet had
the audacity to write Phillips:

> Dear Sir/ — I regret troubling you — but my new
> friend, Tom Wainewright, suggests to me that the
> *nose* in both your portraits of me is too much turned
> *up* — if you recollect I thought so too until you
> argued otherwise — one never can tell the truth of
> one's own features — I should have said no more on
> the subject but for this remark of Tom's — Perhaps
> you will have the goodness to retouch both pictures
> — as it is a feature of some importance — excuse
> my plaguing you with this request —
> yrs. very truly
> Byron

The letter served its intended purpose. I was sacked. To
add insult to injury, Phillips insisted I surrender three pencil
sketches I had made of the poet.

Strange as it may seem — given the Byromania virus
which strikes two or three times a century — my most
memorable recollection of my early days in London centres
on my meeting with the elusive Sarah Wilson, shortly

*EDITOR'S NOTE: A colleague of my husband's — a woman of strong opinions —
has observed that Tom is a consummate belletrist and that he bears a strong
resemblance to the nincompoops Pope satirized in *The Dunciad*! The same
person has cautioned me against providing you with extensive annotation lest
I, like the dunces, parade my ignorance before you.

before her death at an advanced age. Like my uncle's Sarah, this Sarah began life as a housemaid. Early on, she became convinced that the fine folk she served were no better than herself. Once, she even got caught stealing clothes and jewellery from the court apartments of her employer, a lady-in-waiting to King George III and Queen Charlotte. Her plea that she remove them in order to launder them properly fell on deaf ears. She was to be hung, but her employer begged for mercy.

The charming scoundrel was transported to America, escaped the confines of her new master, and using a locket stolen from the Queen, she re-invented herself as Princess Susanna Caroline Matilda, the Queen's sister. She became the toast of aristocratic society in Virginia, both Carolinas, and Georgia, delighting everyone with her vivid accounts of court life. In obvious need of cash to maintain her sumptuous style, she made herself readily open to receiving funds from those in need of royal favour. Money, she assured those who plied her with it, was a necessary commodity to oil the machinery of officialdom, not that she was using any on her own behalf. Her selfless attitude made her a great favourite. Unfortunately, some spoilsport ruined her subterfuge by calling attention to the offer of reward for an escaped bondswoman, who bore a striking resemblance to the Princess.

She was not stymied. She took advantage of the confusion at the outset of the War of Independence to escape to New York City, where she met and married a British officer. She disappears in official history at this point but surfaced in London during the Regency. A hard-of-hearing old trout, she was renowned in her select circle as an example of the hard-won triumph of style over substance, although she had plenty of the latter.

I met her when she sat to Phillips. A gruff but nevertheless warm woman, she asked me, a young stripling, about my ambitions. I told her I wanted to paint faces.

41

"A honourable profession. You will encounter many people of eminence. That will never harm you."

"But I do wonder about the calling. The same face can change its appearance in a matter of seconds. How does one capture the true likeness?"

"There is no such thing, young man. No real likenesses, no real truths. Locke and Hartley have revealed those unsettling truths in their writings. Everything is in flux. You must adapt yourself to that sentiment, the only 'truth' I ever learned."

Sarah was a kindred spirit, who knew the full value of outward appearances. I took my leave, thanking her warmly for her words of wisdom. I felt enhanced by the interest she took in me, her attempt to connect with me, the hapless journeyman.

There is only one other circumstance of note to record concerning my first extended sojourn in London. During my stay at Phillips, I made the acquaintance of one Dora, a servant girl of uncommon beauty. Perhaps it was the soft dewy whiteness of her complexion that led me astray. Or the amber recesses of her eyes. Or the ripe curvaceous flow of her sinewy shape, the essence of womanhood. I wish I could claim she became my Eve, I her Adam. In reality, my role was more of the serpent.

My beloved, a person of uncommon refinement for one of her class, responded warmly to my overtures. Loving too easily and unreservedly, she gave herself to me rhapsodically and was not unduly upset when she proved to be with child.

"Since the child is yours, Tom, I cannot but feel that he or she will be a treasure, a gift of God."

Feigning sympathy for her magnanimous feelings, I nevertheless suggested she do away with it. She could never do that, she assured me, even though she realized she had no claim on me. Suspecting a ploy on her part in which I could be entrapped unawares, I quickly ceased all connection with her.

I must own I was mildly upset to hear a year or two later that Dora died giving birth to a male child, who was sent to Coram's foundling hospital in Conduit Street. Doubtless, he

afterwards made his way into service. My ow
those days was with my own unsteady fortu
direction should I turn in order to make my way in

V

Oscar Wilde offered this sugary comment on the abrupt change of career to which I next subjected myself: "He seems to have been carried away by boyish dreams of the romance and chivalry of a soldier's life, and to have become a young guardsman."

In the full inventory of ensigns in the Bedfordshire Regiment for 1815, my name is misspelled (the "e" is omitted), but even now I would not take it upon myself to correct the Army List. After all, this is one of the few pieces of archival evidence which grounds me accurately in history. In addition, I must confess, I love lists. Some would claim I was a fetishist in this regard. What attracts me to them is their air of mathematical precision and definiteness: they hinder those who pilfer the past and would erase and thus traduce it.

I soon tired of military life, essentially a mode of killing Time and my fellow humans. One biographer has observed that, after only a year, I sold my commission. That this happened a mere ten weeks after Napoleon's escape from Elba led him to conjecture that I was, "perhaps unwilling to be drawn into a European conflict." The implication of cowardice is clear-cut.

The reckless, dissipated life of my companions failed to satisfy the refined artistic temperament I had developed. I made this claim at the time: "Art touched her renegade; by her pure and high influences the noisome mists were purged; my feelings, parched, hot, and tarnished, were renovated with cool, fresh bloom." Under those circumstances, I abandoned barrack-life and the mess-room. I retreated briefly to Linden House. Also, I had become seriously ill. The soldier had been transformed from dashing guardsman to crazed hypochondriac. I was broken like a

43

vessel of clay. "His delicately strung organism," Wilde observed of me, "was most sensitive to pain. He shrank from suffering as a thing that mars and maims human life, and seems to have wandered through that terrible valley of melancholia from which only great souls emerge unscathed. He passed out of the 'dead black waters,' as he called them, into the larger air of humanistic culture."

In all accounts of me, extremes are the norm. Nevertheless, there is one particular piece of slander about my army life I must correct:

> There was one incident in his military life which he still recalled with a strange fascination of pleasure. Since his illness he had taken even more delight in that memory.
>
> He rubbed his beautiful white hands together as he recalled the scene. Some drunken brute of a private had been sentenced to two hundred lashes. He had watched the execution of the sentence from the very first moment to the last. It was the day when he had been taken so seriously ill and had had to resign his commission.
>
> He could see again the white, broad, naked back glistening in the sunlight — the ripple of the muscles under the skin stretched tight on the triangle. And he had seen that white flesh turned swiftly into a raw, mangled, bloody mass. Even now the memory of it thrilled him.
>
> Pain was the expression of human emotion. Not sufficient attention had been paid to it by artists. Those old medieval torturers must have been geniuses in their own way. He would like to have known them. They never experienced pain themselves; they only administered it — uniquely. They were artists playing upon that wonderful, nerve-tangled instrument — the body, with its infinite capacity for suffering.

This dribble is an excerpt from a consummate piece of pulp about me by one Ladbroke Black in his novel, *The Prince of Poisoners* (1932). You will notice immediately that this person is not a historical novelist of any distinction. Also, the writer has obviously confused me with one T.E. Lawrence. And Lawrence's repressed homosexuality and fascination with masochism have been subtly blended with this junk novelist's own morbid interest in the tortured body of Saint Sebastian. In addition, my sexuality has been called into question. I have become the vehicle by which a writer of trash (or pastiche) can comment — somewhat obliquely — on sex and violence. If they want to titillate, these scribblers think it fine to employ me.

What I did actually write about this dark period in my existence:

> *The phantom of fear is always about you. You feel it in the day in every turn; and at night you see it, illuminated and made more horrible in a million fantastic shapes. Such feelings can be resolved into the single word hypochondria; but how much of the inexplicable and astonishing does this word include — and how inexplorable the labyrinth, to the entrance of which it leads.*
>
> *My hypochondriasm is, in reality, the faculty of extracting, for my own use, the greatest possible quantity of poison from every circumstance of life. I have often been pleased in planning to myself the manner in which I could kill such or such a person, or set fire to such or such a house without being discovered. Not that I have ever observed in myself the smallest desire to commit these actions, but they occupied my imagination, and I have often fallen asleep over such thoughts.*

From early on, the diagnosis of "hypochondriac" has been dismissed by those who have written about me and the word "psychopath" has been substituted for it. This is

45

a clever trick by second-rate biographers: seeing a situation they do not understand, they re-invent it to suit their own purposes. My ability to feel rotten about the circumstances of my life and thus "poison" my own existence and, in the process, imagine poisoning someone else has been taken as self-incriminating. If he felt or imagined committing crimes, he must have acted on those sentiments. So the argument runs. My own disclaimer — *"not that I have ever observed in myself the smallest desire to commit these actions"* — has been ignored.

In addition, all compilers of mini-biographies of me (e.g., *Chambers*, *DNB*) as well as those who have written of me at great length are at a loss to account for 1815 to 1820. Is there a great secret to be revealed? If I were a liar, I could claim a stint in Turkey or service with the East India Company. The truth, I am about to divulge, is not glamorous. I simply wandered about London, lost in a thick fog of self-absorption.

I barely managed to pull myself along. I became an outcast, condemned to the company of misfits, especially artists and writers. But artists and writers are rebels. They show how the ordinary in a face, a landscape, or in words can be made extraordinary; they also call attention to their own "specialness" in manipulating the ordinary. No *ordinary* person can love or admire those who show them what they were too ignorant to notice.

Thus, at 22, I returned to the fold from which I had been ingloriously expelled. And, of course, in order to look presentable in the inner sanctums of Regency taste-makers, I had to dress appropriately: braided surtouts, a diamond ring, an antique cameo breast pin, a cambric handkerchief breathing forth Attargul, a pair of pale lemon-coloured gloves, a quizzing-glass, a dark blue coat of military cut, and long brass spurs. The life of George Bryan Brummell, somewhat vulgarly referred to nowadays as "Beau Brummell," bears only a superficial resemblance to my own. However, the foregoing costume, if worn by Brummell, would to this day attract favourable notice. The epitome of masculine elegance, etc. All of these items are seen, in my case, as evidence of dandyism, an inordinate fascination with external appearance.

In 1821, I was daft enough to make this confession to the readers of the *London Magazine*: "*Among my immediate acquaintance, the greatest scoundrel happens to be the man who wears the shabbiest of coats, and the dirtiest of neckcloths; while the best fellow I have the happiness to know is, at the same time, the best dresser, the best looker; to say nothing of his being one of the best thinkers, the best talkers and the best riders — Next to Horsemanship, Dress is my favourite hobby.*" Needless to say, this passage is completely self-reflexive and, not unexpectedly, has been used against me. In sum, I am accused of excessive narcissism. Narcissism + hypochondria = a male hysteric.

Another insult masquerading as compliment: Wilde claimed me as "the pioneer of Asiatic prose." According to him, I "delighted in pictorial epithets and pompous exaggerations. To have a style so gorgeous that it conceals the subject is one of the highest achievements." He then goes on to observe that my criticism is concerned "primarily with the complex impressions produced by a work of art." However, I am accused of being rather dull when it comes to generating "theory," and, he also points out, "he never feels quite at his ease in his criticisms of contemporary work." I plead guilty. As I said at the time, "*Modern things dazzle me. I must look at them through Time's telescope.*"

Although Wilde had a damnable tendency to bestow with one hand and to take away with the other, he did pay me a remarkable encomium — a genuine touchstone in understanding my young life: "This young dandy sought to be somebody, rather than to do something. He recognized that Life itself is an art, and has its modes of style no less than the arts that seek to express it." Amen.

I was at ease with one of the modern masters, little Fuseli, to whom I gave unblinking loyalty. Why? Because he at the very least had the courage of his sordid convictions.

Tiresome, pedantic, learned, the Swissman could never contain himself when enthusing about supernatural forces, so much had they touched his life. "Herr Wainewright, that is the real landscape to which artists must now turn. Enough of this English obsession with fat horses and dull hills!"

"Mr. Fuseli, the English like to look at what can be readily seen by the eye."

That really upset him. "What about the inner eye, the only real entry into nature?"

"You continue to espouse Blake's ideas about inner truths, inner realities."

"What nonsense! He has many interesting ideas, needless to say. But the fellow draws so badly." Like roly-poly, unjolly Mr. Blake, Fuseli, who was truly an outstanding draughtsman, was the only artist in England interested in the phantoms of the night. I like landscapes or canvases filled with rolling hills, yellow and green fields, happy or unhappy rustics; I can even gasp an "O Altitudo" at the majesty of the scenic sublime. But I have always been attracted to chiaroscuro twilight, wherein darkness has the upper hand in the struggle with light. There, bright things battle in vain to assert themselves against the blackness which threatens to annihilate them. In such terrains, I glimpse the central truths of the human soul, of the mixed constituency of good and evil in every human heart.

As it turns out, Mr. Fuseli was more honest than most of us. His *Nightmare* pictures, wherein a hunchbacked simian form sits upon the body of a young sleeping woman, are studies in the contrast between so-called normal and abnormal. Is the ape going to kill or rape the woman? Or is the ape a simple, good-hearted fellow (like Quasimodo) standing guard? If she awakes, will the young woman screech loudly when she beholds the visitor? Does Beast want to harm Beauty? or is he simply paying her a silent adoration? Fuseli had the best questions, a paucity of answers.

VI

I did not have the capacity to become a great artist. Something was missing. Thus, my frequent bouts of melancholia. Despite the limitations that plagued me, I realized my genius found its finest expression as a copyist, one adept at getting inside the heads of other men's creativity. That is a strange enterprise. An act of homage? Perhaps. You certainly have to admire and understand a painter if you are going to copy him. You must be able to look at the world the way he does. If you are a good imitator, you have breathed the same air as the imitated.

When I emulated Gainsborough, for example, I began to see all my fellow humans through a thin gauze covering, their heads, arms, and legs elongated in the most charming and graceful of ways. That painter's celebrated oil sketch — *The Painter's Daughters with a Cat* — assigned to the late 1750s in the catalogue *raisonné* — is my most celebrated invention. According to historians, in the artist's original conception, Margaret, the elder, held a playful kitten in her hands, which Gainsborough later changed his mind about including. In fact I never intended the animal to exist: I wanted the ghost of the creature to reside in the young woman's arms, to give the whole enterprise the look of absolute authenticity and spontaneity. The genius changing his mind, art in the process of being made. That trick worked perfectly: the canvas is in the National Gallery in London.

My research was exacting. I managed to see the celebrated, unfinished oil of the painter's two daughters chasing a butterfly. In my mind's eye, I then aged the two young women by three or four years. I must admit, however, that two relatives of my own — my future sisters-in-law, Helen and Madeleine — sat to me.

Art has a strange way of distorting life. As adults, Margaret and Mary Gainsborough, nicknamed Molly and the Captain by their father, had tragic existences. Margaret, a gifted harpsichordist, flew into a temper when Queen Charlotte expressed an interest in hearing her play. Mary

49

contracted an unhappy marriage to a musician friend of her father; later, she went insane. As you shall discover, my sisters-in-law were the undoing of me.

There's also another side to the life of the copyist: he becomes like an insect burrowing into bark to obtain food. A cruel paradox: the sap of the artist's life may be a necessary ingredient, but eating bark destroys it. I suppose I lacked the originality of a Blake or a Fuseli. Their genius was an insult to the likes of me. They put me in touch with the rage felt by all talented artists when confronted by those who are truly innovative. What was I to do? Simply accept the boundary between the merely good and the supremely gifted? I threw turpentine into the fire: I decided to imitate them as best I could, hoping, very much in the manner of an incubus, to steal their slumbering souls.

Another thing in defence of copyists, forgers, fakers, counterfeiters, and plagiarists. There really is no such thing in art as originality; however, there is always the presence of the past. Painters and writers are obsessed with their predecessors: can I produce a painting or a poem as good as A, B, or C? D was such a genius: what am I in comparison? How can I — thinks X — accomplish anything on my own when I owe so much to Y and Z? X adores Y and Z; X also hates — and would like to murder — Y and Z.

The anxiety of influence is really the fear of becoming a plagiarist. In the manner of a highwayman, Shakespeare plundered the past — so do most other writers — if they are honest about it. *All* works of art are constructed from the living tissue of other writers and artists. At best, then, originality is a hackneyed notion.

What, pray tell, is an "original" work of art? Is such an entity even desirable? Forgive me, but "authentic" and "original" are not allied concepts. The "authentic" work of art — that which moves the beholder — can just as easily be a "fake" or an "original."

The perfect illustration leaps to mind. In the last quarter of the nineteenth century, cemeteries in Boeotia and Asia Minor were ransacked for terra-cotta figurines.

When demand exceeded supply, forgeries made their way onto the market. These artifacts were modelled, baked, then encrusted, often with a black glaze. Sometimes, the copies were not even modelled after genuine figurines.

I never learnt this particular form of imitation, but one came into my hands: a representation of Janus, the double-headed deity. Knowing of the interest of one Mr. Elias Standish in such antiquities, I penned him a letter and told him of the remarkable "find" I had made in my late grandfather's collection. By return of post, Mr. Standish summoned me to his home in rural Hampstead.

Three days later, I made my way there and was surprised to find that the collector's dwelling was a tiny one, of the terraced variety. Mr. Standish himself answered my knock and invited me inside. A tiny, elderly, wizened creature, even shorter and slimmer than myself, he was dressed in a fustian, faun-coloured suitcoat of Georgian elegance. His newly powdered wig was of the kind worn early in the eighteenth century. Although he dressed well, he was obviously a man of no wealth, of no importance in the world.

Thick curtains blocked each window, and, even though my visit was in daylight, I had great difficulty in adjusting my eyes to the darkness that confronted me. Gradually, I became aware of unimaginable clutter. If he had chosen to employ a servant, Mr. Standish would have had difficulty finding room for him because the interior of the house had little or no space even for its owner, who made his way cautiously through tiny tunnels perhaps twenty inches across at best. The interior was filled with Mr. Standish's various acquisitions. Amongst many other objects, I saw at least a thousand Oriental ivories, dozens of Majolica vases, jardinieres, and teapots, two or three dozen ornate carriage clocks, and over one hundred armillary spheres. The elderly man was devoted exclusively to the applied arts, although furniture was not one he cultivated. In all this assemblage, I did not behold any terra-cotta figurines. When I voiced this observation,

51

Mr. Standish thought I way implying I did not wish to part with my treasure to someone who might not sufficiently appreciate it.

"Oh, Mr. Wainewright, I decided some time ago to move into that terrain, an entirely new undertaking for me. I have merely been waiting for the right piece to come along. Never having heard of a sepulchral figure of Janus from Asia Minor, I decided it would be an auspicious beginning. You understand my drift?"

"Indeed, sir." With that, I removed the tiny object from its cloth covering.

Mr. Standish asked if he might hold it. His tiny hands held the object but it was his bright blue eyes which really fastened itself to it, as if consuming it. He was enchanted by the two-headed figurine, at the rendition of countenances remarkably different but joined at the neck. Suddenly, tears coursed down his face. At that moment, I must admit, an enormous infusion of guilt filled me. I considered expressing doubts as to the object's authenticity.

I needed the twenty guineas the collector had offered me, but I was on the brink of depriving myself of the funds, so touched was I by the connoisseur's love of the beautiful, an enterprise to which he had obviously dedicated himself at great cost to all other considerations, particularly his pocketbook.

I was about to betray my entire enterprise when Mr. Standish looked me full in the face. "I can never thank you enough for giving me possession of this treasure, of allowing me to purchase this tiny masterpiece." In that moment, I knew the "originality" of the object was of absolutely no interest to the purchaser. He succumbed to its physical beauty, to its "antiquity," and — if I might venture — its "authenticity." I voiced no objections, took a glass of port with Mr. Standish, allowed him to think me his benefactor, collected my money, and then took my leave.

How did I learn to be a forger? What kind of school of connoisseurship did I attend? The answer is one Stephen

O'Brien, a would-be portrait painter also in the employ of Phillips. About ten years older than myself, he looked like an ordinary enough fellow: tall, well-made, dark. What is often called "black Irish."

What Stephen gained in the ordinariness of his appearance, he gave back in his manner. He twitched badly, his whole body going into frequent and total states of defragmentation. At times, it was difficult for him to hold a brush. He was fond of expletives, often alarming his master's famous customers. In general, he was rage-filled, anger boiling up frequently behind the sitters' backs. His appearance was a contrivance of shambles: loose, ill-fitting trousers and dirty, turpentine-scented shirts. Phillips often warned him about his appearance. His clients, he informed him, did not like to witness ungainliness.

From the start, Stephen decided he and I were allies. I don't think he ever realized quite how condescending he sounded when addressing me, always referring to me in the third person, with the adjective "young" attached: "Young Tom will appreciate..."; "if young Tom would care to see..."; "no doubt young Tom will agree with me that...." Stephen's insufferable manner vanished when he drank, which was often and with considerable brio.

Stephen assumed I was, like him, a malcontent. However, he did not appreciate the fact that I wished to ape the rich whereas he simply wanted to destroy them. He desperately wanted an apprentice. Byron had wanted to use my body; Stephen simply wanted to corrupt my intellect. Once, having imbibed a considerable amount of gin one evening after work, he invited me to his flat so that I could peruse his own work as a painter. For some time, he had hinted that his own canvases were in a completely different — and vastly higher — league than Phillips'. I expected to see some well-turned pieces, perhaps an assortment of landscapes and still-lifes.

Not unexpectedly, his small, dark flat on the third floor of a derelict building off the Fulham Road was inhabited by rodents and large insects. At first, I could take in very little of the contents of the sitting room, so crammed was it with paintings, sculptures, etchings, and display cabinets. Too many to let me examine any one closely. There was nowhere to sit, but Stephen was not at all bothered by such trifles. His energies were concentrated on providing me with a commentary on the strange objects I beheld. I must admit I was not prepared for anything I was shown: the entire contents of the room were from an assortment of centuries, none from our own.

One of the first objects Stephen drew to my attention was a portrait of King Edward VI, a substantial oil on panel, in which the eight-year-old monarch costumed in the magnificent regalia of his office stands defiantly before the viewer. The well-executed picture is from the school of Holbein, the German artist who possessed a most excellent knowledge of the English monarchs. When I exclaimed over the "majesty" of the piece, Stephen shuddered at the awful pun. I asked him how such a piece had come his way. He squirmed slightly, which led his body into a major convulsion.

When that was completed, he smirked, then shrugged his shoulders. "Oh, young Tom might as well know!" This was exclaimed in a loud voice which, this once, allowed the hint of a brogue to escape.

"A while ago, the Master sold me a portrait of a young girl in a rounded skirt which had been in his possession for many years. Not a distinguished piece of work. She held a carnation, meaning it was some sort of betrothal picture. I decided to enhance it. I converted the carnation into a dagger; then I transformed the skirt into an embroidered coat, elongated the girl's forehead, and substituted her cap for the more dashing one the young man is wearing. I left most other things alone but added the king's coat of arms to his right."

"So you changed an unknown girl into a King of England?"

"Young Tom understands. I enhanced the ordinary and manufactured a Holbein."

"But the picture is a fake!"

"What do you mean a fake? It was a commonplace piece. Now it commands attention. Can anything be more authentic?" He paused. "Young Tom is shocked?"

"No." I refused to own up to the very sentiments which overwhelmed me.

Whether he was convinced or not by my declaration, Stephen turned to another canvas, *Christ at Emmaus*, supposedly a Vermeer. In this instance, he had obtained an inconsequential but authentic seventeenth-century canvas, stripped it, and then painted his religious subject in the manner of the Dutch master. He had been careful to use paint constituted from materials readily available in the seventeenth century. A striking etching, *The Mocking of Christ*, by Lucas van Leyden was so well done that its mastery of detail surpassed that of the original.

I was shocked but tried not to reveal it. I questioned the older man on his methods, on his attention to every conceivable angle of detail. I made a number of small objections, but he had answers prepared for any obstacle that I could throw in his way. Finally, I took a different approach. Why bother?

Certainly not for financial gain, I was assured. Stephen had no intention of selling his copies, of passing them off as genuine. In fact, he had never even been tempted to pursue such a route. The filled-to-bursting room confirmed this statement. What is more, Stephen did not like — even admire — the artists he copied.

He himself seemed puzzled by my question. He did not even have a prepared answer. "I suppose," he began. Then stopped. Finally, all he could muster was: "I suppose it's the challenge." He realized that this was unsatisfactory. He tried again: "If it's so easy to manufacture these things, it shows how the artistic impulse is essentially mechanical. The right chemistry, the right paper, etc. There may be no such thing as inspiration."

Having gotten that far, he went on: "Shows us that all these objects," he now waved his hands in the general

55

direction of the contents of the room, "are mere contrivances to please the rich."

"But you must love the originals if you spend so much time copying them? You are entering into the spirits of their creators?" At that moment, the room seemed eerily dark, only a small lamp giving a strange illumination to the treasure horde.

Stephen became furious. "Young Tom does not comprehend. My talent is mechanical. Being such, it gives proof to the essential sordidness of the artistic enterprise. Artists like Phillips are mere connivers in bed with Mammon."

For Stephen, there were no objects of beauty, only corrupt sinners like himself who produced its appearance. Even then, I could see he hated himself for what some might call his God-given capabilities. For him, those powers were Satanic.

That night, Stephen's eyes gleamed in rage. Then, his body was attacked by a mighty convulsion. Quite soon, he settled himself on the floor, his body drained of all its nervous energy. At this point, I took the opportunity to ask if he would instruct me in his "calling." He assured me he would do so, provided I purged myself of the notion of art's sanctity. I agreed.

Many years later, after my apprenticeship had been completed and Stephen drifted back to Ireland, I realized he had tricked me that evening. He had deflowered me, shown me an essential truth about the place of art in the world. So thoroughly Catholic was he that he could never offer his imitations for sale, but he wanted to engage someone to commit such sins by proxy. He did not possess Faust-like ambition. Stephen also lacked killer-instinct, although Mephistopheles had decisively stolen his soul.

My catalogue *raisonné* (pre-deportation) is remarkably slender. Here is the inventory as compiled by one art historian:

1. *Amorous Scene*. Pen and sepia wash. 11 x 14 3/4, unsigned. British Museum. Laurence Binyon, *British*

Museum Catalogue of British Artists (1907), IV. 249:
"A park of undulating ground with thickets; a tall
lady with a sunshade is moving away from the
foreground, looking with scandalized or envious
eyes at a couple seated on a bank (left) and ardently
embracing; in the background, among the thickets,
three other pairs of lovers are similarly engaged. All
are dressed in the costume of the period (about
1820). Perhaps an illustration to a story."

2. *Subject from the Romance of Undine, Chap.* V. Oil. 22
   x 35, signed. Exhibited at the Royal Academy,
   1821. Whereabouts unknown.

3. *Paris in the Chamber of Helen.* Oil. 18 x 27, signed.
   Exhibited at the Royal Academy, 1822.
   Whereabouts unknown.

4. *An Attempt from the Undine of De la Motte Fouque.*
   Oil. 11 x 14 1/2, signed. Exhibited at the Royal
   Academy, 1823. Whereabouts unknown.

5. *The Milk-maid's Song.* Oil, 5 ft. 7 ins. x 4 ft. 7 ins.,
   signed. Exhibited at the Royal Academy, 1824 and
   the British Institution, 1825. Whereabouts unknown.

   Mr. Palmer, one of Blake's young disciples in
   those days, well remembers a visit to the Academy
   in Blake's company, during which the latter pointed
   to a picture near the ceiling, by Wainewright, and
   pronounced it "very fine." (Gilchrist, *Life of Blake*
   (1880), ii. 42).*

---

*EDITOR'S NOTE: One of my husband's esteemed colleagues — some people
consider him a pedant — has insisted I mention Tom was one of the great
poet-illustrator's patrons. Copy X of *Songs of Innocence and Experience*
was commissioned by Wainewright, who had it bound in boards covered
with light green calico. A contemporary of both men states: "It was
executed by the highly gifted artist expressly for his friend Mr.
Wainewright, to whom, I am told, he was at the time under considerable
pecuniary obligations."

6. *First Idea of a Scene from Der Freischütz.* Oil, 3 ft. x 2ft. 6 ins, signed. Exhibited at the Royal Academy, 1825. Whereabouts unknown.

7. *Sketch from "La Gierusalemme Liberata."* Oil, 5 ft. 5 ins. x 4 ft. 8 ins., signed. Exhibited at the Royal Academy, 1825. Whereabouts unknown.

8. *Portrait Sketch of Helen Frances Phoebe Abercromby.* Crayon, 10 x 8 3/4, signed. Present whereabouts unknown. Reproduced as frontispiece to Wainewright's posthumous *Essays and Criticisms.*

9. *Portrait Sketch of Madeleine Abercromby.* Crayon, 10 x 8 3/4, signed. Present whereabouts unknown.

Except for the frilly little pastiche inspired by Fuseli that now resides in the British Museum, the remainder of my known early work is in the collection of "whereabouts unknown," a first cousin of "anonymous." However, the situation is not as desolate as it might seem. Many canvases of mine, under the signatures of others, are held in some of the finest public and private collections. Here, then, is a summary of my real portfolio.

CANALETTO. Heaps. Many in the collection of Her Majesty.

GAINSBOROUGH, *Thomas.* Quantities of drawings, mostly portraits of snooty-nosed aristo ladies. You already know the history of the oil sketch of Mary and Margaret.

MORLAND, *George.* Thick impasto, stables, landscapes, peasants — never really tried with these. At least five.

REMBRANDT. Crucifixions, beggars, interiors, etc., etc. Two hundred or so. Some paintings, a dozen drawings, the remainder etchings.

ROWLANDSON, Thomas. Fat ladies, piss pots, messy boudoirs. Over thirty (unchallenged) in the Rowlandson catalogue *raisonné*. It never ceases to amuse me that the artist himself — who did not die until 1827 — authenticated several examples of his work undertaken by myself. You have to be a particularly adept forger to convince the supposed creator of the genuineness of the work you seek to pass off as his. Or was Rowlandson envious of the work he beheld? Did he recognize a greater artist than himself, someone he was not worthy of — certainly someone who paid him an enormous compliment by deigning to imitate him? Did Rowlandson lie?

STUBBS, George. Big-bottomed mares with their foals. (One splendid example is in the Mellon Collection at Yale.)

My Rembrandts once got me into a spot of trouble. I passed two particularly splendid etchings off on that difficult, fastidious Milanese-born, naturalized Englishman Paul Colnaghi, the print dealer. The provenance was clear: the collection of my late grandfather. Two weeks later, he summoned me to his inner sanctum on Berkeley Square where my Rembrandts had been joined by six or seven others, all of the same time period.

"Take a good look, young man," he commanded me. "Your two and the remainder are very different, yes?"

"Indeed, they are sir."

"So you can see the discrepancy, yes?"

"Indeed, sir. Where did you get the others?"

"Where else would Colnaghi obtain items for sale? From the best sources, yes?"

"That may be true, sir, but in this instance you have been unfortunately cheated."

"Colnaghi is never cheated, yes?"

"I hesitate to contradict one of your eminence, but in this instance — and in my own self-regard — I must sadly do this. Notice how much fresher, more rich the ink hits the page on the two I sold to you. My grandfather was a man of consummate taste, a true connoisseur. The two I sold you are choice productions, not of the humdrum variety of the others in this chamber. One might even venture to suggest these others are the work of a forger."

Mr. Colnaghi became apoplectic. "That is a ridiculous suggestion, no?" He removed an inordinately long cloth from his trousers in order to wipe his now sweaty brow, and, playing for time, he took his time attending to his face. Finally, he allowed a tiny smile to cross his face. "In art, inspiration is everything, yes? Artists are better on some days than others, yes? The pull from the plate is better, the paper slightly better, yes?" With that, he rang the tiny bell on his desk and a servant came to fetch me.

Turnaround is fair play, but I cannot help being a bit angry at Henry Fuseli, who claimed my erotic drawings as his own. In fact, one connoisseur accused me of having fathered the obscene drawings of Fuseli. To *that* charge, I plead guilty. Those offspring were taken from me by the little Swiss, who, in one case, dated a drawing 1809, rather than 1818. He thus appropriated it to his canon. In the catalogue compiled by the inestimable Gert Schiff, it occupies number 1620: *Symplegma eines Mannes mit drei Frauen.* (Man having sex with two women.)

Another would-be taste-maker loved these drawings, although he did not suspect that they were of my devising:

> These obscene drawings are among the finest of
> Fuseli's works, and they possess an extraordinary
> atmosphere, where the faces of the actors are quite
> unmoved by the strange actions which they
> perform; Fuseli's hair-fetishism appears in the
> elaborate headdresses of the women, whose hair,
> poured and moulded into fantastic shapes, suffers no
> disturbance from the static violence of which they
> partake. My only regret is that I am unable under
> our present dubious legal system, to reproduce
> several of them here in their entirety; all that I can

do is give some details from six of these drawings lately in my possession.*

As practised in the twentieth century, there are two main variants in the dominant mode, the cinematic: *soft* or *dry*, wherein a couple is nude, their bodies joined; they writhe, they achieve orgasm — no genitals are displayed; *hard* or *wet*, wherein every minutiae of coupling is on display, but the man, as he reaches the threshold of ecstasy, removes his penis from the vagina and ejaculates. In the former, the moment of orgasm is invisible; in the second, the moment of rapture is masturbatory. In the former, you see nothing; in the latter, you see something which would not ordinarily happen. Pornography, unfortunately, has fallen on hard times. Luckily for me, I was born in the age of true pornography (pre-photography), where absolutely everything was faked: the artist's imagination was, as it should be, the source of the rendition of all sexual activity.

My drawings are neither wet nor dry. It is difficult to have wet drawings, although that rascal Blake depicted *putti* shooting off jets of milky dew from out of tiny little penises. Unfortunately, pornography no longer contains a shade of ambiguity, nor is it susceptible to a variety of interpretations. However, all pornography, I now happily realize — as a man and thus biologically biased — is about the power of the penis (whether absent or present), for which biological contraption Partridge has countless synonyms. There are relatively few for the pudenda.

A spirit has lived too long when he is not synchronous with the wet dreams of his age.

---

*EDITOR'S NOTE: The same repressive legal system still operates (*vide* poor Robert Mapplethorpe), and my publisher has forbidden me to reproduce *Symplegma*.

VII

My melancholia continued unabated. I felt unfulfilled. This was my sad reflection: *"In short, when a fellow reaches twenty-seven, there is a crowd of bitters behind him; and the field for delightful hope to disport in is dwindled to a mere span before him."*

In the above passage, I was not very specific about my life as a painter-forger. Until about the age of eighteen, I resided with my uncle at Linden House. I ventured into London for short stays, sometimes of a week or more. After the Army, I stayed with my uncle once again, renewing my courtship of London. In those days, the city was an even stronger mixture of refinement and crudity than it is today. Piccadilly Circus had just been formed (1819) by the intersection of John Nash's magnificent and pristine Regent Street with the more pedestrian and emporium-filled Piccadilly Street. The Great Stink of 1858 was still far in the future, but even then the stench of the river was so bad that the exteriors of some residences were draped in sheets soaked in chloride of lime.

My only successful employment was as a forger. I felt a sham, an empty vessel. I began to drink heavily. Then, suddenly, my talents as a writer were recognized by John Scott of the *London Magazine*, who requested me to put down on paper some of the expressions of feeling to which I had been excited by the work of Raphael and Rembrandt. Mind you, the reflections that Scott heard had been prompted more by the help of spirits than by oil on canvas. With some modification of plan (only two tumblers of gin rather than the usual six), I cheerfully obeyed him. It struck me as somewhat ridiculous, that I, who had never authorized a line — save in Orderly and Guard Reports (and letters requesting money — should be considered competent to appear in Scott's prestigious magazine.

For Scott, I became Egomet Bonmot and in my first appearance presented my *Modest Proposal of Service*: *"Without fear of controversy, then, I affirm myself to be Sir*

Oracle fit for every thing, prepared for all accidents: ready to pass from grave to gay, from lively to severe; to sigh in concert with the woods that wave o'er Delphi's steep; — in a word, Sir, I hereby pronounce myself to be, not one, but all mankind's epitome." For that magazine, I produced a rich harvest, under the pseudonyms of Janus Weathercock and Egomet Bonmot, viz., *Janus's Jumble*, Ego's *Much Ado About Nothing*, Janus's *Private Correspondence, Intended for the Public Eye.* If pressed to choose one passage as the epitome of my talent in the essay form, it would be this observation on the Venetian Tintoretto's wondrous canvas, *St. George Delivering the Egyptian Princess Sabra from the Dragon:* "*The robe of Sabra, warmly glazed with Prussian blue, is relieved from the pale greenish background by a vermilion scarf; and the full hues of both are beautifully echoed, as it were, in a lower key by the purple-lake coloured stuffs and bluish iron armour of the saint, besides an ample balance to the vivid azure drapery on the foreground in the indigo shades of the wild wood surrounding the castle.*" Here, I manage to find the proper literary equivalent to the imagination of the visual artist. Can a critic aspire any higher? Wilde thought not: "Wainewright's conception of making a prose-poem out of pain is excellent. Much of the best modern literature springs from the same aim. In a very ugly and sensible age such as ours, the arts borrow, not from life, but from each other. He — not Coleridge — is the greatest of the English critics. We must aspire to be his loyal sons." So the entire Aesthetic Movement — Art for Artifice's Sake — is my invention. Wilde's attribution is eminently correct. No falsehood there.

Any description I have seen of so-called literary "circles" makes them sound quaint, oozing the comforting air of gentlemen's clubs — port being passed around the table after the ladies have withdrawn. They are, in reality, much more like uneven triangles. A likes B's poetry and has given public testimonial to the genius of B; A subsequently finds merit in C's verse, whereupon B takes offence because no one who likes his verse could admire C's miserable efforts. This results in a circle of confusion, wherein envy and jealousy are activated: A becomes a castaway. Put another way: for literary circles to attain any measure of success, there have to be those who are "in" the circle keeping others "out," the border between the two continually shifting. Battle lines — and then swords — are drawn.[*]

As I have hinted, life within literary circles can be not only dizzying but also hazardous. At a dinner party at Charles Lamb's (he of the homicidal sister), I once sat across from De Quincey of opium-eating fame. He was polite, even though he seemed in a black depression. On that occasion, he thought me a person of "unaffected sensibility" beneath a veneer of "affectations of manner"; later, he took back any suggestion of a compliment when he insinuated he would have never reached such a conclusion had he known the heart of murderer beat within my breast.

My new patron Scott was a deeply melancholic, bitter, nervous, frowning man, short in both height and intellect. Not a showman, he fancied himself a ringmaster. His authors had to tow his line or risk falling from grace. I showed a measure of independence and was quickly pushed

---

[*]EDITOR'S NOTE: Sadly, I know from first-hand experience the kind of conflict Tom is describing. My inability or unwillingness to conform to the expectations of high school cliques led to ostracization. In recent years, I have witnessed from a distance another dismal battle. Day after weary day, my husband tells me how traditional literary historians like himself are being routed by the theorists, now the kingpins in the academy.

Recently, at a reception at Massey College, a graduate student told me of a new war zone. Years ago, there used to be a discipline called "Commonwealth Literature," which referred to the writings of the English-speaking residents of Canada, Australia, New Zealand, the Caribbean, Africa, and Asia — all those places which had been or were still under English rule. Then, much to this young conservative's dismay, the term vanished and was replaced by "Post-Colonial," the idea being that the residents of the former colonies were striking back, producing a literature that condemned their former oppressors. Having explained this turnaround in considerable detail, the student observed that "Post-Colonial Literature" was a phenomenon highly approved of and supported by the powerful monolithic Modern Language Association, the corporate headquarters of which is in New York City. An ardent Canadian nationalist, Ms. Wu is disgruntled. "It's all a sham," she assures me. "The bloody Yanks are colonizing us all over again, but it's politically incorrect to say so publicly."

out of the inner circle. He used the mask of seriousness to unsuit me. He did not care, he announced, to publish writers who were merely witty or sophisticated. He silenced my facetiousness — the source of my acumen as a critic. As quickly as he had bestowed favour, he withdrew it.

This tragic event was followed by Scott's death in a duel. Not unexpectedly, it was a literary quarrel. Wilson and Lockhart of *Blackwood's* had labelled the stable of the *London Magazine* as the "Cockney School," suggesting their writing was vulgar and commonplace. An outraged Scott retaliated, venomous words were exchanged, a duel was arranged, and eventually Scott met his end on 16 February 1821 from the pistol of a fellow editor, one Jonathan Henry Christie. Strange to die because of an adjective!

The dying Scott was taken to Chalk Farm Tavern, where, as it happened, I witnessed his final moments. Poor fellow! Even now I feel, as if it were yesterday, round my neck the heart-breaking, feeble, kindly clasp of his fever-wasted arm — his faint whisper of entire trust in my friendship — the voice dropping back again — the look — one stronger clasp!

Commentators on my life have dared to question my assertion that Scott died in Chalk Farm — they insist he expired at his lodgings on York Street, Covent Garden. The suggestion is that I was furious that Scott had dropped me; then, filled with a dose of guilt at his passing, I tried to insinuate that I had been a loyal friend to the end despite Scott's hostility to my writing. This is not the case. I was there: I obviously know. And what is more, the death of a contemporary made me acutely aware of my own mortality.

My hypochondrial phase gradually gave way to an exceptionally early and agitated mid-life crisis. And so I retreated to the countryside where *"the short tender grass was covered with marguerites — such that men called daisies in our town — thick as stars on a summer's night. The harsh caw of the busy rooks came pleasantly mellowed from a high dusky grove of elms at some distance off, and at intervals was heard the voice of a boy scaring away the birds from the newly sown seeds."* As you can readily discern in this snippet, I have always been a lover of the countryside. This led to Oscar Wilde's seemingly cruel observation, which I am certain he intended as a compliment: "Like most artificial people, he had a great love of nature."

So far, I have given you an overview — the topography — of my life history. Soon, we shall be immersed in all the nitty-gritty of the Wainewright murders. Before taking that turn, I must make you acquainted with some further facts. I have been quite candid — at the considerable risk of being found reprehensible — in confessing to you the sordid truths of my deprived childhood and unsettled youth. I have highlighted my indecisiveness, hypochondria, lack of ambition, and feeble talent. I have been markedly unsparing in self-flagellation. How many autobiographers have been willing to confess so freely how they made messes of their lives?

I was a man drawn to inaction, an unsettled mass of confusions. But nothing in my early life history suggests a villain, much less a serial killer. Those persons who become the scapegoats of history are palimpsests into which lesser beings can inject their own choices in poison. I was and remain a self-centred, vainglorious man. I plead guilty to being a simulacrum, a moral cipher.

Allow me — in an admittedly digressive vein — the indulgence of defending myself in a new way. My affection for animals is part of the public record of my life. But it has taken a curious turn in all accounts of me. I am described as being feline. Sometimes, the context is neutral. W.C. Hazlitt: "Wainewright gathered up the floating flappets of his frock coat, treading as gingerly as a cat among china." But quickly things turn nasty. John Scott: "During a tiresome argument, Tom began to rap me on the head, as one sees a cat deal with an elderly kitten which retaineth its lacteal propensities over due season." Then, it is assumed, some references I have made to myself as feline can only be seen in a negative context: "I trusted, by this time, to have got upon my subject, as the composers say, but my will backs as obstinately as a cat."

My love of dumb creatures has been used against me in even viler ways, especially when my name is placed next to that of Eugene Aram, a near-contemporary of mine, by Havelock Ellis, so-called expert on the criminally insane. Like me, Aram has been immortalized. In his case, a ballad by Thomas Hood and a novel by Bulwer-Lytton.

In 1745, when Aram was schoolmaster at Knaresborough in Yorkshire, a man named Daniel Clark, his intimate friend, after obtaining a considerable quantity of goods from tradesmen, disappeared. Suspicion of being involved in a swindling transaction fell upon Aram. His garden was searched, and some of the goods were found there. However, because there was insufficient evidence to convict him of any crime, he was discharged. For several years he travelled through parts of England, acting as usher in a number of schools, and settled finally at Lynn, in Norfolk. During his travels he had amassed considerable material for a projected comparative lexicon of the English, Latin, Greek, Hebrew, and Celtic languages. He was undoubtedly a brilliant linguist, who recognized what was then not yet admitted by scholars, that the Celtic language was related to the other languages of Europe and that Latin was not derived from Greek. But he was not destined to live in history as the pioneer of a new philology.

Thirteen years later, in February 1758, a skeleton was dug up at Knaresborough, and some suspicion arose that it might be Clark's. Aram's wife had often hinted that her husband and a man named Houseman knew the secret of Clark's disappearance. Houseman was at once arrested and confronted with the bones that had been found. He insisted he had no knowledge of the recently discovered bones, but he confessed that he had been present at the murder of Clark by Aram and then gave information as to the real place where Clark's body had been buried. A new skeleton was dug up, and Aram was immediately arrested and sent to

York for trial. He was found guilty and condemned to be executed. While in his cell, he confessed his guilt and asserted that jealousy — not greed — had motivated him to kill Clark, who had seduced his wife.

In his account linking me to Aram, Ellis tells how this vicious malefactor, having killed Clark, returned to the scene of the grisly murder in order to set free a canary for fear that it might starve in its cage. The bird is an incidental detail in Ellis's narrative, but he takes the opportunity to suggest a link between myself and Aram: both men displayed sentimental attachments to animals that masked a venomous hatred for their fellow creatures. Once more, guilt by (weak) association.

VIII

In 1820, I retired to Mortlake, near Barnes, a squat riverside village, an extension of London on the Thames. I settled on that spot because the great alchemist, John Dee, who had resided thereabouts in the sixteenth century, commended it as a place of extraordinary beauty. There, I soon began to experience the subtle pleasures of rusticity.

Almost immediately, however, a series of new dilemmas confronted me. My landlady was a native of Turnham Green, Mrs. Abercromby, who had once been a Miss Weller. Firstly, she had married a Mr. Ward, by whom she had two children: a boy (who died as an infant — I never asked his name) and Eliza Frances. Ward was evidently a niggardly drunkard, who regularly brutalized his wife. After Mr. Ward had the misfortune, in an alcoholic haze, to fall down a staircase and break his neck (there is a family legend that six-year-old Eliza, at the top of the staircase, held her arms out to receive dear papa, withdrew her welcome embrace and jostled her father just as he reached her, inadvertently causing him to lose his balance), the desolate widow affianced herself to Lieutenant A, whom she had known slightly for about six months before her husband's untimely passing. This match yielded two daughters, Helen and Madeleine. Unfortunately, the lieutenant passed away after siring these two.

By the time I encountered her, Mrs. A had squandered her Weller inheritance. From the army, Mrs. A received an annual pension of £10 each for Helen and Madeleine. From their maternal grandmother, these two received £30 each year. Mrs. A's other income, from scattered real estate, amounted to another £100. So it was that she took in the likes of me. Eliza, whose high spirits had never been a pleasure to Mrs. Weller, had been disinherited. The old lady once claimed (improbably) that Eliza had placed some noxious substance in her dish of tea.

Mrs. A's large home fronting the Thames was ostentatious bordering on grand. The rooms were crammed with possessions, every inch of space rigorously ordered. She had no taste but had once had a great deal of money. The result was predictable enough: a lot of fifth-rate paintings by first-rank artists, Chippendales and Hepplewhites whose proportions had gone wrong at the factory. It was difficult to walk through the house, so encumbered were the passageways with small tables, wash stands, and chairs of various sizes.

Mrs. Abercromby was a huge mountain costumed in silk dresses of overwhelming brightness, fuschia being her favourite colour. Her silks came from the most prestigious London merchants. Not a diligent landlady, she was too used to looking after herself. Her various coiffures took up a great deal of time. Some days, luxuriant auburn tresses flowed down almost to her backside. On others, her hair piled up on itself in mound upon countless mound, would have made her a suitable lady-in-waiting at the court of the Sun King.

Mrs. Abercromby's complexion was subject to many fluctuations: high coloured on some days, matte white on others, the latter obtained through liberal dosing of zinc oxide. She could not finally establish her person: an aristocrat-refugee from some foreign court or a woman who did not mind dropping liberal hints that she was a frail creature of the flesh. Similarly, her conversation fluctuated between extremes of grim condescension and merry flirtation.

Occasionally, she made peremptory inquiries on my health or on my various peregrinations in the neighbourhood. Helen and Madeleine, eleven and ten at the time, were sweet-natured enough little damsels, often fighting with each other for supremacy in my affections. An other-worldliness clung to both of them, I noticed. They did not really play together. Madeleine followed the instructions of her slightly older sister, who supervised her in a supremely bossy way.

Not surprisingly, my attention was almost entirely focused on Eliza, then seventeen, who was neither friendly nor forthcoming. At first, I thought her a shy beauty who needed coaxing. I must admit that Eliza's delicate features — her clear brown eyes, upturned nose, delicate chin intrigued me. I wanted to break down that barrier of reserve.

One day, when Mrs. A and the children were paying a visit to the old parson and his wife, I made my advance on Eliza by penetrating her front flank, i.e., I embraced and kissed her. A bit to my surprise, she yielded at once. Soon we had retired to her chamber, where, my unsheathed helmet standing at full erection, she issued various unlady-like requests as to how and where she wanted to be serviced (*viz.*, my Tasmanian composition, *The Reunion of Eros and Psyche*, where Eros roughly cups Psyche's ample breasts and extends his tongue deep into her mouth; at the same time — not as visible as it should be — Eros is ramming his beloved's back entrance). All of these entreaties were issued by madam in a matter-of-fact, military manner. Only when I had expended my seed did it dawn upon me that I was not the first soldier to have been enrolled in the lady's service.[*]

---

[*]EDITOR'S NOTE: I am not puritanical — and at the risk of being accused of being prurient I have not censored Tom's lurid descriptions of his sexual exploits — but I am deeply bothered by how Tom and Eliza conducted themselves at Mrs. A's home, which was also the residence of two young girls. I certainly never engaged in heavy petting — much less intercourse — in my parents' home, even though Stephen did attempt to lead me down that particular garden path. I "gave" myself to him only on our wedding night.

Eliza and I never fell in love, but I soon realized that she was full of ambition, a quality I singularly lacked. She wanted to live in London and to have a place in the literary demi-monde. Above all, she wanted to experience the luxuries of this world, especially in contrast to dull Mortlake. She did not have it in her to live in the provinces, develop the semblance of a deranged imagination, and then attempt an escape. I soon realized that she could be a useful coadjutor to me. If I were too soft, her hardness would redress the balance.

Thus, our relationship was launched on a note of genuine compromise. The understanding we reached is illustrated in this verbatim account of a love spat which began when I became jealous of a past attachment.

Tom: You are angry with me?

Eliza: Have I not reason?

Tom: I hope you have; for I would give the world to believe my suspicions unjust. But, oh! my God! after what I have thought of you and felt towards you, as little less than an angel, to have but a doubt cross my mind for an instant that you were what I dare not name — a common lodging-house decoy, a kissing convenience, that your lips were as common as the stairs —

Eliza: Let me go, Sir!

Tom: Nay — prove to me that you are not so, and I will fall down and worship you. You were the only creature that ever seemed to love me; and to have my hopes, and all my fondness for you, thus turned to a mockery — it is too much! Tell me why you have deceived me, and singled me out as your victim?

Eliza: I never have, Sir. I always said I could not love.

Tom: You say you cannot love. Is there not a prior attachment in the case? Was there anyone else that you *did* like?

Eliza: Yes, there was another.

Tom: Ah! I thought as much. Is it long ago then?

Eliza: Many years ago, Sir.

Tom: And has time made no alteration? Or do you still see him sometimes?

Eliza: No, Sir! But he is one to whom I feel the sincerest affection, and ever shall, though he is far distant.

Tom: And did he return your regard?

Eliza: In his own way.

Tom: What then broke off your intimacy?

Eliza: His position and pride of birth.

Tom: Was he a young man of rank, then?

Eliza: His connections were high.

Tom: And did he never attempt to persuade you to any other step?

Eliza: I cannot betray him.

Tom: Tell me, my angel, how was it with him? Was he so very handsome? Or was it the fineness of his manners?

Eliza: It was more his manner: but I can't tell how it was. It was chiefly my own fault. I was foolish to suppose he could ever think seriously of me. But he used to make me read with him — and I used to be with him a good deal — and I found my affections entangled before I was aware of it.

Tom: And did your mother and family know of it?

Eliza: No — I have never told anyone but you!

Tom: Why did he go at last?

Eliza: We thought it better to part.

Tom: And do you think the impression of him will ever be erased?

Eliza: Not if I can judge of my feelings hitherto.

Tom: May God forever bless you! How can I thank you for your condescension in letting me know your sweet sentiments? You have changed my esteem into adoration — Never can I harbour a thought of ill in thee again.

Eliza: Indeed, Sir, I wish for your good opinion and your eternal friendship.

Tom: And can you return them?
Eliza: Yes, to the furthest limits of my ability.
Tom: And nothing more?
Eliza: No, Sir.
Tom: You are an angel, and I will spend my life, if you will let me, in paying you the homage that my heart feels towards you.

A bit icy. That's how I'd describe even my early days with her. She never asked me questions about myself, but she quizzed me incessantly about my prospects and my friends. Perhaps the most effective way for me to tell you about my relationship with her is to show you the exchange of letters which passed between us when we were courting. Distressed by Eliza's intolerable behaviour towards her family, I had absented myself to London for a fortnight to collect myself.

Madam,
I offer tender apologies for my abrupt departure the other afternoon. I very much enjoy the pleasure of your company and remain much amazed, as I have told you countless times before, of how never having been to London, you have acquired a remarkable knowledge of its peculiar ways. Yours is not only a fertile imagination, but one intimately acquainted with the sometimes bizarre ways of the world. When I am with you, I am filled with admiration at the dexterity of your remarkable mind. Of course, the beauty of your person is beyond compare.

My departure, precipitous though it may have been, can, I think you know, be accounted for by the remarkable displays of temper to which you have turned of late in the direction of your mother and sisters. You obstinately call Helen and Madeleine "half-sisters," but I know these young women are entranced by you, hanker to address you by the title of "sister," a privilege you refuse them. As for Mrs. A, she is often of the mildest disposition though occasionally "willful" as you label her. To be truthful, I am sometimes fearful you will turn your displeasure at poor Tom, so smitten with you that he will be destroyed by such ill treatment. I must needs escape to protect myself from such a turn.

I cannot bear to be away from my sweetest kitten for too long, but I hope she will think of poor Tom's nervous leanings, his aversion to any show of temper. Believe me, Madam, your most obedient and affectionate servant.

Sir,
Your missive has just reached me. My mother immediately demanded to know the contents of said document, stating that she had the right to read any piece of writing which graced her residence. I refused, telling her that the letter was not so much intimate as discursive on the state of the arts in the metropolis. She called me a liar and, in a great huff, absented the room. Sir, you have no real idea what I endure here. You think my half-sisters pleasant little girls. Maddy is demure and refined enough, though dense. Helen does not possess the same disposition. She has an unfixed nature, which she conceals. She possesses a true villain side. In fact, she practices mendacity to an elaborate degree. She has caused all manner of trouble to other children who attempt to befriend Maddy. In one instance, less than a year ago, she contrived to have a poor wretch of a servant boy dismissed because Maddy preferred him as a playmate to herself.

Sir, I am a prisoner here. Sometimes, I do strike out against my wardens. My poor spirits simply become overwhelmed. Only then do I lose my bearings. This is not constitutional, would never be directed against a person of your refinement and charm.

I long for news of London. Whom have you seen? where have you been? When will you once again grace us with your presence? Yours, with true regards

Dear Eliza,
Your letter brought me much comfort. You must endeavour to reign in your sometimes unseemly displays. Such manifestations are foreign in London, where any display of anger is clandestine. Here, you may possess high spirits but never display them. If you join me here, you must allow yourself to be tutored in this regard. Surface, you will learn, is everything.

Allow yourself to be seduced by the pleasures of London. Just the other day, at the Royal Academy, I saw "The Crucifixion" of Rembrandt for the first time. Magnificent in its realization of the magnificent nude body of Christ, the blood streaming down his face; his wounds gaping wide, the god-man suffers the fullest tortures to which human flesh can be subjected. I also took tea with Mr. and Mrs. Blake the other day at Fountain Court, a street filled mainly with grim warehouses. Their two-room flat is completely encumbered with the little genius' oeuvre. They showed me variant copies of the same illuminated books, some hand-coloured by William, others by Catherine. She prefers much brighter, radiant hues. Indeed, her renditions are superior to her husband's. You will also enjoy the many pleasures of the emporia here, some displaying elaborate pyramids made of pineapples, figs, and grape; one china merchant has tableware set out as if a splendid dinner party was in progress. One must be careful to stay adrift here, as there are many gin intoxicated wretches abounding the street. Bread is often in short supply to rich and poor.

My dear puss, I hunger for you.

Sir,
You are correct. The Eliza to whom you have expressed warm feelings is my true self. Allow your mind to rid itself of all previous displays of temper. I long to be with you, to share the joys of our great capital. Yours obediently,

Dearest,
… You are of a firm constitution, much more so than your poor wretch, Tom. You have enough resolve for the two of us. You are the tigress queen, who has ensnared my heart. With undying love,

Sir,
Join me at your earliest convenience.

Not highly sexed perhaps, but Eliza appeared to be a wonderful creature. I was convinced I had finally discovered the perfect Cleopatra to my Antony. In addition to consoling me during the lonely hours of the night, I was certain I had found in her a kindred spirit. By necessity, the life of a forger is an exceedingly lonely one, but when, within a year of our settling in London, I asked her to be my helpmeet in this endeavour, I immediately discovered she was more than adept at following instructions in this rarefied branch of art. In that regard, she proved a satisfactory wife.

IX

As soon as Eliza and I found and settled into lodgings — those on Great Marlborough Street once inhabited by the great actress, Sarah Siddons — suitable to the comfort and aspirations to which we were entitled, we became nuisances to each other. By inclination, my wife, despite her earlier protestations to the contrary, had no interest in literature although she had a goodly comprehension of it. Most of my friends and acquaintances were preoccupied with the artistic impulse, in themselves and others. What makes a man become a writer or an artist? What drives someone to render experience into a whole new order of existence?

Hazlitt's fascination with the phenomenon of Napoleon — the way in which this tiny lump of a man attempted to reorder the European continent — bored Eliza. My friend's infatuation with his inamorata, the difficult Sarah Walker — which drove him to the edge of madness — gained none of her sympathy. De Quincey she found common. "I am supposed to maintain polite conversation with the son of a linen merchant?" she asked one day. I pointed out that he had a truly astounding intellect. I vouchsafed my opinion that his fascination with how the injuries and injustices of childhood find expression in dreams would make his reputation as one of the greatest of the English critics. She denied my enthusiasm, although she once told me that his essay, "On Murder Considered as One of the Fine Arts," was an astute piece of writing.

The frequently hand-to-mouth existences of the members of my circle must have frightened Eliza, making her uncomfortably aware that my sideline as a counterfeiter propped us up financially — but in an increasingly precarious way when the art market experienced poor sales. Instead of any interest in chit-chat touching on the vagaries of the creative instinct, my wife's attention began to be focused on the activities of the underworld, those creatures who crudely connived at tricking others out of what was rightly theirs.

For hours, she would enthuse — to anyone who would listen to her — about common cheats: the "Snoozers" who slept at carriage stations and then made off with the luggage of distracted travellers; the "Snow Gatherers" who stole clean clothes off the hedges of the wealthy while a maidservant was momentarily distracted; the "Bluey-Hunters" who removed lead from the tops of houses; the "Skinners," those infamous women who enticed children into an alley way and then stripped them naked. I remember both De Quincey and Hazlitt staring in unconcealed amazement as my new wife regaled them with such anecdotes. Why has Tom married a common creature interested only in such mundanities? their countenances proclaimed. I was embarrassed, caught as usual in the middle.

If I tried to distract Eliza from such interests, she became morbidly silent. Usually, she would simply leave our sitting room. As I pondered the matter, I realized I had the obligation to tutor my beautiful, uncultured wife. I had fallen in love with her outward perfection. Now it was my obligation to give her a mind worthy of that beauty and of my intellect. Although, as I already knew to my cost, Eliza could be obdurate, I was certain I had the power of a Pygmalion to form my beloved to my own specifications.

Unfortunately, my statue was already alive, possessed of a mind of her own. Quite soon, she began to answer me back, convinced I was a pupil in need of her instruction!

"You and your associates are much too naive about the real state of the world," she suddenly informed me one day.

"Naive? We strive to understand the real spiritual underpinnings of the universe," I countered her.

"There are no 'spiritual underpinnings.' What pompous expressions you mouth! The world exists as we behold it. There is nothing else."

As you can imagine, I was irritated to be lectured at by an uneducated young woman from the provinces. "Madam, I am not speaking of religious belief but of the mysteries that surround life itself."

"Well, if you wish to maintain such assurance in the face of daily experience, you are welcome to it." On that occasion, she rose, gathered herself up, cast an ironical glance in my direction, and withdrew to the bedroom.

The simple truth, I soon realized, was that Eliza was bored. Moreover, London had simply not lived up to the expectations with which her fantasy life had for so many years imbued it. She needed distraction, had to be exposed to more than the bear-pit kind of entertainments to which she was drawn. Her imagination — and thus her expectations — had to be lifted.

Years before, when I had first settled in London, I had been deeply touched by witnessing the great Mrs. Siddons as Lady Macbeth. What if Eliza were exposed to such a potentially metamorphosing experience? Having given her "farewell" performances to the stage many years before, the actress, without benefit of costume or stage props, occasionally "read" an entire play herself, acting all the roles. When I saw the announcement of one of those rare evenings, devoted to *Macbeth*, I suggested we attend. "If you wish to, Tom," was my wife's half-hearted response.

A tall, comely woman, Sarah Siddons attended to every detail of her Lady Macbeth. When I first saw her, she had abandoned the traditional white satin dress of this role and substituted shroud-like white drapery, the more easily to suggest the frightened ghost-like creature that the hard-nosed heroine of Shakespeare's tragedy eventually becomes. The actress's powdered headdress, in the Greek manner, was meant to remind the spectator that the Scottish chatelaine was a spiritual descendant of Antigone and Clytemnestra. This Lady Macbeth may have been consumed by ambition, but she was also a most beautiful, feminine, fashion-conscious creature, one corrupted by exterior forces. When she tells Macbeth, "Glamis thou art, and Cawdor, and shalt be / What thou art promised," her countenance and frame and voice were filled with an exalted prophetic tone.

This woman, the spectator realized, knows the future. She controls Macbeth perfectly, but then her own sense of guilt and vulnerability take over. Her "O, O, O" at the end of the "perfumes of Arabia speech" was not rendered as a mere sigh, but as a convulsive — almost sexual — shudder.

It was ten years since I had seen Siddons when Eliza and I attended her reading at the Oddfellows Hall. As usual, the actress was dressed in white and her hair was still rendered in the Greek fashion. Unfortunately, during the intervening decade, the actress had become unduly portly. She was now a creature of immense size, of almost comic proportions. Behind the screen in front of which she was placed, there was a light, which made it appear as if two extremely large people inhabited the stage.

As the lighting in the hall darkened, Mrs. Siddons began in an awkward, almost subdued fashion. Then, suddenly, the actress seemed to inhabit each of the characters whose words she uttered. No longer was her unseemly appearance a distraction. I felt as if carried back to the earliest days of the theatre, as if transported to ancient Greece itself. The woman before me was a priestess, perhaps the muse incarnate. She remained in the one spot, her shadow now whirling behind her as she moved her head or moved her hands. Greed, ambition, evil, and guilt lived on that stage. In every sense, the actress, as she grew older, had enhanced her understanding of the tragic sense of existence.

I was taken out of myself that evening, scarcely able to breathe at some moments so transfixed was I by what I had beheld. As we made our way out of the hall and onto the street, I could hardly contain myself. Eliza, I noticed, was silent but not in a reflective way. I made some stumbling remark about how Mrs. Siddons' acting had improved vastly since her retirement.

"I shall have to take your word for that," she briskly assured me.

"Were you not transported by her grandeur, by the way in which she could show so many emotions?"

"She is a simple conjuror, Tom. She practises all kinds of slights of hand in order to reproduce those feelings."

"Yes, I know she is the mistress of her art. But there is

more to it than that. There is a common humanity that breathes through every line as she utters it."

"Your mistake, my dear Tom, is that you have never learned the difference between illusion and reality. The power of any artist is in the conniving, in the manipulation of the audience. I thought her 'machinery' creaked badly. She is a bad artist because her subterfuges are too easily discerned, even by a country bumpkin such as myself."

"I could see no creaks."

"I'm sure you saw none because you did not look for them. I wonder if you even know *how* to look for them. An actor is really a form of mountebank. He connives an impersonation in order to dupe an audience. He must not allow his methods to become obvious."

"But perhaps you were only looking for the contrivances and, thus, that is all you allowed yourself to behold."

"You may be correct, husband. But you have a fatal flaw. You consider an actor actually has to feel the emotions she renders. That is your tragedy. No, I am certain that acting and believing are two different things, to be kept quite separate from each other."

"But any artistic impulse is a manifestation of our real selves," I heatedly rejoined.

"'Real selves'? What does that mean? No. You are wrong. Art comes from manipulation. It is not derived from suffering, from loss, from personal misfortune. Really, you have always lived your life in accordance with *my* principles, but you have never had the courage of your own convictions. You adhere to a strange psychology of the Lockean variety. Of course, if you wish to believe in the power of the subterranean, I would not wish to hinder you."

She paused, a thin smile crossing her face. "I often think you have little knowledge of yourself, Tom. Of your own real powers." She paused. "You claim to be an 'exquisite' but your understanding is often merely commonplace." Having delivered herself of that insult, she retreated into her habitual silence.

My wife's unwillingness — or inability — to respond

with any sort of feeling to Mrs. Siddons disturbed me, as did her cynical views on the nature of art. I said nothing more that evening, although my wife's increasing coldness in every conceivable aspect of our life together grated on me. What kind of a helpmeet did I have?

About a month after Mrs. Siddons' rendering of *Macbeth*, I encountered the tragedienne at a small gathering at Leigh Hunt's. I introduced myself to her, immediately allowing how transported I had been by her performance. I also mentioned that my wife and I inhabited her former lodgings.

"Indeed, sir, I am much beholden to you for your kind remarks. It gives me great satisfaction that my waning powers continue to move others." She bowed, in a tidy and comely fashion.

"Madam, I had seen you at Drury Lane in role of Lady Macbeth many years before. I think your rendition is now more powerful."

She seemed startled but gratified. "Many would disagree with you."

"May I venture a question? When you render Lady Macbeth, do you inhabit those feelings you project so forcefully?"

"Sir, that is a difficult question. I used to attempt to grasp those vexatious emotions but — to be honest — my mind is usually on the mechanics, on how I can display an emotion. I know the words perfectly, but my attention is centred on the accurate projection of their meaning to others. That is my dilemma. One has to become a bit of a conniver. I am merely a conduit, a halfway house between the Bard and the audience. A poor vessel such as myself must struggle to say afloat amidst the storm at sea." With that, she nodded her head in my direction, smiled broadly, and took her leave.

Stumbling along — that is how I would describe my marriage to Eliza. Things kept on a relatively even keel as long as we agreed to disagree. Money concerns began to intervene more and more. The market in forgeries depleted, mainly because so many talented artists could not sell their original paintings and turned to forgery to keep the bailiffs from their doors. In 1827, the now-pregnant Eliza and I were forced to retreat to Linden House, to the comforts of my uncle's abode. It was then that the threads of history — and of infamy — caught me in their iron grip.

X

Unfortunately, we must now venture into a new terrain, that of my supposed malefactions — the so-called Wainewright murders, those of my uncle, my mother-in-law, and, the most celebrated of all, my sister-in-law, Helen. Most accounts work from cause to effect. Although not a piece of fiction, my story proceeds from effect to cause. And that is precisely the task to which I must now turn.

You have been kept waiting a long time. Am I a poisoner? You are sophisticated enough to understand that nothing in life is ever yes or no. There are mixed bags, foul ups, muddles, cock ups, balls-ups, failures to communicate, innumerable moments of catastrophe. This is the part of my story which has never been told. All criminals have portmanteaux full of alibis and excuses. I shall offer none of them. I shall provide something completely different: a context.

Since I have placed myself on trial, you must permit me to act in my own defence. Together let us sift the evidence and interrogate the past. In turn, I shall permit you to be a severe judge, but I shall expect at least a modicum of open-mindedness, a willingness to allow the past to be modified by the present.

So far, you have seen my life as a mosaic. Now, you shall have to gaze carefully at a series of still lives. When you look at work in that genre, for example, it seems to tell the truth. But what is left out of the painter's rectangle of vision can be more significant than what is within it.

We'll examine all the events leading up to the infamous deaths, but for the moment let's go forward to 1830, whereupon having insured herself for £12,000, Helen died mysteriously. We'll concentrate for the moment on the initial set of circumstances surrounding her death. I'm sure you'll agree with me that, by any reckoning, the surviving evidence about her strange death makes no sense. Why would she insure her life if she was not a willing victim? Helen was very much aware that Eliza and I were desperately short of funds: why would we spend a small fortune (over £200) in premiums needlessly and then do her in, at which point we would be the obvious suspects? Look carefully at the chronology. How fully am I implicated in what happened?

25 March 1830

I call at the Pelican Office and ask if I could secure a policy of £5000 for two years on the life of Helen.

1 April 1830

Eliza and Helen call on Monkhouse Tate, the secretary of the Pelican, to complete the formalities. Premium still unpaid. Later that day, Helen calls alone at the Globe Insurance Office to propose a policy of £5000 for two years on her life.

3 April 1830

Helen and Eliza return to the Globe, where Helen is examined as to her reasons for wishing to secure such a policy.
   Helen: "I am desired to do so."
   The Globe secretary: "Why?"
   Helen: (demurs)
   Eliza: "It is so. There are some money matters to be arranged. Ladies do not know much about such things."

The Globe, aware of the application at the Pelican, turns Helen down.

5 April 1830

At the Alliance Helen is severely tested by one Mr. Hamilton, who receives the proposal, and who is not satisfied by her statement that a suit is pending in Chancery, which would probably terminate in her favour, but that if she should die in the interval, the property would go into another family, against which contingency she wishes to provide. The young lady becomes piqued: "I supposed what you had to enquire into was the state of my health, not the object for insurance."

To which reply Mr. Hamilton, with a thoughtful look, says: "A young lady, just as you are, Miss, came to this very office two years ago to effect an insurance for a short time, and it was the opinion of the Company she came to her death by unfair means."

Helen replies: "I am sure there is no one about me who could have any such object."

Mr. Hamilton replies gravely: "Of course not," but adds that he is not satisfied as to the object of the insurance; and unless she states it in writing, and the directors approve it, the proposal could not be entertained.

8 April 1830

Helen and Eliza make their second appearance at the Pelican Office. After drinking dishes of tea, they pay the premium of £51.9.2d plus (this was in every way a properly conducted legal transaction) stamp duty. Helen proffers two banknotes: one for £50, the other £10.

15 April 1830

The sisters (rather out of breath and worse for wear) present themselves at the Eagle Office. The policy for £3000, secured on 30 April, is no longer sufficient. Helen bargains for another £2000. This proposal is turned down. The two then make their way to the Hope (a well-named firm), where they solicit a policy for £2000 for two years.

19 April 1830

With flying colours, Helen passes the examination conducted by the medical officer at the Hope. Later that day, I accompany her and Eliza to the office of the Provident. Helen asks the Managing Director, Barber Beaumont, to issue her a policy of £2000 for two years.

27 April 1830

Policy with Hope Office completed.

There are some exceedingly strange inconsistencies in how the above chronology has been employed in the various accounts to which I have been subjected. Does it contain irrefutable proof that I plotted to poison Helen once I had inveigled her into insuring her life for thousands of pounds?

Consider the following:
1. I appeared at the offices of the various insurance companies on only two occasions.
2. Helen actively sought to have her life insured.
3. The firms which accepted premiums from Helen were well aware of startling inconsistencies in her assertions as to why she wanted (or needed) to purchase policies from them. They, as their subsequent actions demonstrate, accepted her money with the hidden proviso that they would not pay up if — for some reason — she were to die within two years. Their crimes are compounded by their resolve that, in the event the beneficiaries (or someone hired by them) did away with Helen, they

would fight to have those persons convicted and thus deprived of ill-gotten gains. Experts at stealing candies from babies, they might be said to have incited a murder.

part two
Helen

My narrative will be much shorter, simpler, and unadorned, more straightforward than Tom's — certainly devoid of my brother-in-law's convoluted flights of fancy. My story has to be plainer: I am a woman, and women are seldom as flamboyant as men. My life history does not have a plot: it is a straight line stretched to the point of complete invisibility. No geometry, no circles, no triangles.

In all accounts of the Wainewright poisonings, I am merely a corpse or a woman just about to become a corpse. Tom had all the pretensions, all the glory. As murder victim, I would welcome slightly more publicity, although I was from childhood informed that the wish to be noticed was a sin.

When I was alive, I learned that lesson all too well and, as a result, I am, in all the accounts, merely the violated body. As such, I have no personality. To a large extent, no right to exist. Perhaps a right to be murdered? Yet the mysterious circumstances of my death led to Tom's being tried for forgery. Alive, I was a nonentity; in my death, I was an excuse for revenge. Not much of an existence.

I was begotten when my mother, the redoubtable Mrs. Abercromby, was married to Mr. Ward but having an affair with dashing Lieutenant A. Mr. Ward fell down the stairs and died (I doubt Lizzie pushed him — she was never quite the *dea ex machina* she claims to be). My mother married my father. I have no recollection of the mysterious Lieutenant, who took flight when my mother was pregnant with Madeleine.

My mother, a single parent who endured two pregnancies within twenty-one months, was both harsh and remote. Mrs. Abercromby — I never felt any inclination to call her "Mama" — did not like children, and she was sorely disappointed when four pregnancies yielded a still-born son and three daughters. If she could have gotten away with it, she would probably have left me or Madeleine by the road to perish. Or drowned us, like unwanted kittens.

Mrs. Abercromby was an abandoned woman, but she, in turn, abandoned her daughters. We were valueless, by-products of her infatuation with two men. My suspicion is that she had little sense of herself, felt some self-esteem when valued by men, but, because of her own sense of worthlessness, was unable to mother us. In her scheme of things, all women — herself included — were of no value. During my entire life, I lacked the words to describe the horrors I witnessed.

In our tall, slender, and dark house of innumerable bedrooms, we had a cook, a maid, a footman, and, briefly, an under-footman. My mother had little to do but fret, usually about the boarders whose rent kept our finances precariously afloat. My first painful memory is of a heated fight between mother and a maid, who left later that day. Usually, my mother moaned, snarled, and — when these failed — screamed. As young girls, Maddy and I became so accustomed to mother's moods that we often hid from her. Lizzie, very much the eldest child, knew how to read mother — and to manipulate her. She had the ability — an uncanny one — to disappear just as mother was about to "blow" (Lizzie's word). So Maddy and I got to bear the full force of each storm.

Lizzie was a miscreant, although one of the silent variety. She wasn't disobedient or naughty or rebellious. She wasn't *apparently* any of these things. There would be a fire in the kitchen, but no obvious explanation of how it had been set. Cook had been out of the kitchen for ten minutes, during which time a block of wood would spontaneously combust. Or one of my mother's prized pieces of porcelain would lie broken by a fireplace, apparently thrown to the floor by the maid while she was dusting. Events like these would lead to yet another of mother's miserable tantrums and the dismissal of yet another hapless domestic.

To Maddy and myself, Lizzie was usually cordial. She was ten years older than us and, when we very little, we worshipped her. Especially, we admired her cool poise around mother, of whom, unlike us, she was never frightened. Maddy and I were never talkative, but we could, if necessary, speak. I am sure that this is the reason why we were never involved in any of our half-sister's pranks. I suspect Lizzie was afraid of tattletales.

Imagine two silent girls wandering a house in tandem. They speak to each other, but most of their energy is consumed by watching others, waiting for something — anything — to happen. Imagine further two little girls whose beige-coloured dresses merge into the heavy, stolid colours of the rugs, drapes, and furniture. Imagine even further frizzy-haired Lizzie — costumed in pink, green, and lavenders — stealthily gliding in and out of the same rooms.

Perhaps you are familiar with Gainsborough's oil of his two daughters, Margaret and Mary, chasing a butterfly? The younger one stretches her arm out to touch the insect whereas the older girl is a bit more hesitant, as she clasps her sister's hand. Maddy was always more impulsive than me; I was the sister who had to keep things under control. Or perhaps you have seen the less well-known *The Painter's Daughters with a Cat?* In that double portrait (*pace* Tom, undoubtedly the work of the girls' loving father), the older girl looks out at the spectator a bit warily and with her left arm holds her sister back. The younger girl is more dreamy and slightly more curious, as if she is trying to size up a situation. She is not as reserved as her elder guardian spirit.

From our earliest years, Maddy and I shared a room with Lizzie. This can be stated more accurately: Lizzie allowed our small bed to occupy one corner of her bedroom. We were squatters, who were allowed a little space by a charmless despot. Lizzie did not exact any rent, not even a vow of silence. We were her small audience. She was our Sarah Siddons.

Maddy and I were never noisy. We couldn't be — this might annoy one of the paying guests. Lizzie's high spirits were, at times, encouraged by mother, who knew that the antics of some children were considered engaging, could help to create the "family" atmosphere so necessary in running a profitable rooming house.

My second memory has to do with Lizzie. I was four, she almost fourteen. One night, when Maddy and I had been sound asleep, the door to our bedroom opened. Through half-shut eyelids, I could see a very dishevelled Lizzie lighting a lamp. Her white nightgown, badly torn, was covered with blood. She removed the garment, threw it to the floor, and then, naked, frantically searched her chest of drawers. After a minute or two, she pounced on a piece of linen rag and then tried to stem the flow of blood from her vagina. Gradually, she seemed to be satisfied that the bleeding had stopped. She looked over in our direction and assured herself that we were fast asleep. I could see copious tears falling from Lizzie's red, swollen eyes. Frightened, I grasped Maddy's hand.

It's only me: Eliza. It's not my turn yet, and I promised Helen I
would not interrupt. But I must insert a few words here. Unlike
Tom, Helen is not a liar. But she gets everything wrong. She also
carries plainness in verbal expression to the outer limits of
bathos. She makes simplicity a vice.*

*Regarding our common mother, Mrs. Abercromby. She was
a ginger-haired, full-figured woman. What is sometimes still
called Rubenesque. She was a woman of appetite. She certainly
took a great delight in love-making.*

*I have almost no recollection of Mr. Ward, but my five-
year-old's remembrance of Lieutenant Abercromby is of a tall,
well-made twenty-five-year-old, at least ten years younger than
mother. I never saw them making love, but I do recall the two of
them — in a very undressed state — hastily pulling their clothes
on when Mr. Ward, my father, arrived home unexpectedly.
Lieutenant A's enormous engine hose and mushroom cap was
still at attention, its head the same cherry red as his face.*

*Helen's "second" memory is accurate, but it doesn't go far
enough. When I was fourteen, Lieutenant A — after an absence
of almost five years — returned home. He was now Mr. A,
having divested himself of his military title. For a few days,
mother was a happy woman. I didn't recognize my stepfather
until I heard one of the maids use his surname. Then a vestigial
memory of having once known our new boarder asserted itself.*

*When I asked Momma about Mr. A, she had no hesitation
in divulging the truth. Mr. A might return for good, but while he
was making up his mind, she didn't want Helen or Maddy to
know he was their father. Also, if Mr. A asked me to "comfort"
him, I should do so.*

*Comforting Mr. A was no easy matter. For a few days, I
was asked to perform trivial tasks. I carried glasses of port and
freshly laundered shirts to his room. Then, one afternoon, Mr.*

---

*EDITOR'S NOTE: As you can appreciate, I was startled when Eliza's voice first
interrupted Helen's. Eliza's aura is much stronger, seemingly more dominant than
her half-sister's, and I simply had to surrender to her "broadcast" — I obviously
had little choice in the matter. To distinguish her interruptions from her sedate,
lady-like sibling's story, I have placed Eliza's pronouncements in italics.

A told me that he had problems getting his "thing" to its proper size. Why this should be of any concern to me was puzzling, but the remedy was easy enough. I simply had to put my hand on "thing," conveniently located underneath his trousers. Then, we both gasped with amazement as the fabric miraculously expanded and stretched at my magic touch.

This game, which seemed harmless enough, satisfied Mr. A for a few days. I found this activity predictable and boring. So did Mr. A it turned out, as he suggested that I might want to see what "thing" looked like. I wasn't very curious, but Mr. A assured me I wanted to look at it. He quickly removed his trousers and undergarments. This time, he touched his engine — which looked like an engorged turkey neckbone with sinews still attached — and started moving his hand back and forth over the head of his "little man" who had, Mr. A assured me, a funny way of talking. Mr. A's own speech had now become slurred, and his face now took on a strange, haunted expression. As his breathing became more laboured, he told me that some drops of angel dew would soon come out of the mouth of "little man," my "new toy." Mr. A was exactly right and, shortly afterwards, told me I could leave his room.

This new activity went on for a few more days and itself became predictable and routine. Then, Mr. A asked me if I would like to taste "little man's" dew, which he told me had a peppermint taste. So fellatio soon followed, although the bitter, dank, seaweed taste of his semen bore no resemblance to the promised candy. A few days later, these pleasures no longer sated Mr. A, who — lying completely naked on his bed — ordered me to remove my clothes. With his large and strong hands on my hips, he forced me to mount his "spike." I was not prepared for what happened. When he shoved his penis into me, it felt as if shards of ground glass had been inserted into my vagina. I screamed. With one hand, Mr. A grabbed my buttocks and lifted me up and down as if I were a rag doll; with the other, he cupped my mouth so that no sound could issue from my throat.

My menarche followed a few days after the rape but, somehow, the two events have been fused together in my mind. Mr. A penetrated me only this once. He left Mortlake a few days later. Momma was furious. She blamed me. She never mentioned Mr. A again.

Helen, the daughter of Mr. A the malefactor, may be determined to play the role of some demented Clarissa Harlowe, but it was her father who transgressed my person.

I am sure that Lizzie is telling *some* of the truth. I am reasonably sure that she had sexual congress with many of our house guests, but I am also certain that my father, Lieutenant A, was not one of her partners. From the Army Ordnance, my mother received a pension of £10 a year for Maddy and me; this money was granted because Lieutenant A died in 1812, when I was three! Not only did Lizzie want me dead but now, still unsatisfied, she wants to remove any semblance of good opinion I may have of a father I cannot remember.

The experience I witnessed might well be the onset of Lizzie's menarche. With her — and with Tom — truth has a curious, exceedingly short life. Their truths are only relevant to their immediate needs, desires, and wishes. For them, truth is never an end in itself, only a means to another end.

I am not sure there is much to tell of the next six years. Maddy and I went to dame school and became proficient in reading and writing. We also received instruction in drawing and music. I remain a reasonably good pianoforte player but have never (even now) mastered the harp.

Since I possess — and intend to share with you — a huge inventory of Tom and Lizzie's wrongdoings, it is incumbent upon me to confess my own frailties in a straightforward manner. I was very attached to my younger sister, perhaps inordinately so. Never wanted by my mother and shunned by Lizzie, I clung to Madeleine. Obviously, I have no memory that predates her. She was always there and, even as a young child, I assumed the role of surrogate mother to her. In the role of Madeleine's translator, I found consolation. The result was that I gained a companion to share my misery. I was also very

95

possessive. Nor was I completely accepting of my child. I guided, chastised, and, sometimes, punished her. Compliance was my goal and in that endeavour I was, up to a certain point, remarkably successful.

The first rub was when Madeleine became attached to Rebecca Hoyle, a child of her age, whose mother, Mrs. Hoyle, was our neighbour at Mortlake. Better situated than us in both finances and rank, this hypochondrial lady became the object of my mother's avid pursuit. Even more bad-tempered than my own poor excuse for a parent, Mrs. Hoyle was an obese but nevertheless whirling creature of unseemly ambition. In her middle thirties when we encountered her, she was also tremendously stupid, just as some people can be deeply superficial. So much of both commodities can exist in some people that the excess might pass for a virtue. But not in this instance. Mrs. Hoyle's home was filled with large, garish imitations of Chippendale, unlike my mother's which were genuine. Whereas Mrs. Hoyle owned wretched copies, Mrs. Abercromby possessed worthless originals. My mother's friend's clothing was in the Chinese mode then fashionable. On her, the delicate, frail colours and subtle lines of those costumes were unseemly at best.

When we visited the Hoyles, there would always be a shower of unpleasantries rained on the various servants. Some remnants of dust were seen on this or that table, the tea was always weak, the cake not sweet enough. As their wont, the servants apologized and withdrew, scampering away as soon as possible from their ever-complaining mistress. I wish I could say Rebecca was like her mother, but such was not the case. She was cheerful, friendly, eager to please, and affectionate. A beautiful, frail-looking child, she smiled easily and often. Her clothing was of the finest materials, cut plain. I have a good memory of her flaxen curls, her large, deeply blue eyes, and skinny little frame. I wish I could remember Rebecca ever slighting me. She liked Maddy and myself immoderately, taking great pleasure in our company. I wish I could claim that she preferred Maddy to me and thus ostracized me. If anything, the opposite was true.

What more can I say? I hated her. If my heart was tugged in her direction, so might be Maddy's. Deeply suspicious of such good nature, I decided to eliminate it from my sight.

Alone with my mother one afternoon, I asked her what a "vixen" was.

"A female fox, child. Surely, you know that!"

"Yes, mama. Does the word have other meanings?"

"Why should you ask such a foolish question?"

"Because you are not a female fox, and Rebecca told me that her mother had referred to you as a vixen."

My mother tried not to look startled. "Indeed. Said she more?"

I looked down, refusing to meet my mother's eye.

"Speak up when you are spoken to."

"Yes, madam."

"Said she anything else?"

"Yes."

"And what was it she said?"

"I was not sure of the words."

"Surely you remember some of them?"

"Perhaps. I'm not certain." I paused, as if trying to imagine words not in my vocabulary. "Some of them were 'insufferable,' 'intractable,' 'vainglorious.'" Mother paid close attention now, her eyes scanning my countenance for the shadow of a lie.

"You are a foolish child, Helen. Imagining things that do not exist." She gestured that I should leave her presence.

The next week we did not receive the Hoyles. On the day Mrs. Hoyle routinely came to drop off the card announcing her "at home," the manservant was instructed to say Madam was not at home and that he was without authority to receive such a card. My ploy had worked perfectly. Mrs. Hoyle and her daughter did not visit us again.

My second endeavour was just as successful. A year later (and about a year before Tom's arrival), mother engaged a boy — an orphan from Coram's on Conduit Street in London — to work as an under-footman. More the height and build of a six-year-old than the ten years he improbably claimed for himself, and bearing the ill-effects of malnutrition, Theo was desperately eager to please. Like many of his class, he loved his oppressors, having absolutely no idea that those above him were in any way using him to advantage. In other words, he was happily down-trodden. His daily chores were vast and cumbersome. He rose at half past five, cleaned the clothes and cutlery and lamps, got the parlour breakfast for the other servants, lit the pantry fire, cleared and washed breakfast, got properly dressed, got parlour lunch, opened the door when any visitor came. After lunch, he took the candles and lamps up to the drawing room, drew the shutters, took glass, cutlery, and plate to the dining room, laid the cloth for dinner, took the dinner up at six sharp, assisted at dinner, brought the things down again at seven, washed them up, brought down the dessert, got ready the evening tea, took it up at eight, brought it down at half past, washed up, took down the lamps and candles at half past ten, and went to bed at eleven.

All this was done with alacrity and enthusiasm. Since he could not read, he had no way to amuse himself, although he had a single indulgence: a small runt of a white mouse to whom he fed table scraps. He was attached to this vermin, allowing it to share his bedding.

I am ashamed to say that Theo was equally fond of both Maddy and myself. Sometimes, he would wink at us behind mother's back — or allow a smile to cross his face if he came across one or both of us on the stairs. Maddy became fond of that puny boy. One day, I heard her inquire about the mouse. Theo allowed a hint of pride to escape his lips when he described some trick he had taught the rodent to perform. Soon, Maddy would steal below stairs to visit both owner and pet.

Once again, I had encountered a rival for Maddy's affection. A rival more difficult to put away as even my mother was cognizant of the flair Theo brought to his wide range of tasks. Another important consideration was the paltry sum she paid for all those services. So, I must own up, a series of fires soon took over the relative tranquillity of our lives: I had borrowed a page from Lizzie's sordid book. These conflagrations always occurred in rooms where Theo had just been. A pattern asserted itself, one which my dullard of a mother could glimpse. The boy was dismissed. No direct accusation was ever made, but my mother refused to give him any sort of testimonial. On the day of his departure, I saw him take off on foot, a heavy knapsack on his frail back, a little cage of twigs in one hand. His knock-kneed frame set off warily. He never looked back. I gazed after him until he disappeared down the lane.

As we got older, my sister and I existed on the fringes of Lizzie Ward's life; we remained the afterthoughts of our mother. We were the audience; they were the performers. No one saw us. In fact, we didn't want anyone to notice us because that always led to trouble.

We were ten and eleven years old when Tom descended upon Mortlake. I have to forget about what he later became in order to write of the initial impression he made. We had never met a man or woman like him. I wouldn't want to give you the mistaken impression that he was kind or generous or considerate. He bustled, moved quickly, talked with his hands, could not get words out of his mouth quickly enough. Sometimes, I thought he would choke on his own thoughts, so anxious was he to transform them into words. He declaimed like a demented thespian, a sort of comic Hamlet who is unable to cease soliloquizing. Tom was always busy noticing things and, immediately, commenting on them. He never stopped, as if he were a mechanical doll whose spring never exhausted itself.

Mrs. Abercromby was overwhelmed by someone more self-centred than she was. Tom spoke of Maddy and me to her. He noticed us. We were surprised, but really, it turned out, we were excuses for his flights of fancy. For example, he once complimented Maddy on the green satin ribbon she wore in her hair. This led to a declamation of about ten minutes on the joys of childhood innocence ("Regardless of their doom, the little victims play"), the significance of the colour green (spring, renewal, rebirth, naivety), Laurence Sterne's addiction to that colour, and, finally, Tristram Shandy's pursuit of the insane Maria.

Tom was a life force. I am not sure that is always a good thing. In short order, he launched himself into our dull lives and also into Lizzie's bed, not a difficult task.

I have to speak up yet again. I don't want to be an encumbrance, but you can see for yourself how Helen will use any opportunity to deprecate me. I am not — and have never been — promiscuous. I have had what some people might consider a reluctant attitude towards the body. From my teenage years, I was very intrigued by the idea of having sex, but I never liked performing it. Somehow, the experience was always unsatisfactory, the desire only intermittently rampant, the orgasms faked.

Mrs. Abercromby was aware that I had coition with some of the boarders. I never received money, but these men would sometimes present me with little gifts, tokens of esteem.

I'll ignore Lizzie's outburst. My entire life was interrupted, used, and cannibalized by my half-sister. It is not my task to describe Tom's whirlwind courtship of Lizzie — Tom has already provided you with those details.

Tom arrived in 1820. My mother, born in Turnham Green, had met both Mr. Griffithses — Tom's grandfather and uncle — on several occasions. She was the cousin of one Samuel Weller Singer, a friend of Tom's. When Tom arrived at Mortlake, he was surprised to discover that his landlady knew his grandfather, his uncle, and one of his friends. Startled might be the more appropriate word.

The dalliance (I am sure that is the correct word) between Tom and Lizzie began soon after his arrival. My half-sister, who had been routinely absent from our bedroom once or twice a week, no longer made any pretense of sleeping there. Four months passed. Tom and Lizzie vanished. Mrs. Abercromby informed Maddy and me that the pair had married and moved to London. I am not sure that Tom and Lizzie ever went through any formal ceremony to solemnize their relationship.

I do know that I did not see either of them for almost ten years. I did not want to have anything to do with them. Maddy and I remained at home. Gradually, we took over the management of the boarding house from our mother. Business declined.

In addition to the pensions paid to Maddy and me, my mother owned other houses, the rentals from which yielded another £100 a year. Maddy and I also shared an annuity of £30 from our maternal grandfather. In 1828, my mother unwisely made a loan of £200 from one James Stewart, an unscrupulous Scots rent-collector. When we were unable to meet our annual payment of interest, the greedy Stewart forced us to sell the Mortlake house.

We had nowhere to live, but my mother now had over £1500 in ready cash. She wrote to "Mrs. Wainewright" who, by return of post, urged us to visit Linden House, where she and Tom had settled in 1827, two years before. As Lizzie was not the most dutiful of daughters or sisters, we were startled at this invitation, no less surprising, as through one of our relatives, rumours of Tom and Lizzie's waning financial resources had reached us. We had also heard that Lizzie had given birth to a child, a boy. Maddy and I were certain that the Wainewrights wanted to get their hands on the proceeds of the sale of the Mortlake house. In this instance, the extent of our paranoia was far too limited.

We arrived at Linden House on 5 March 1830, a week before I reached the age of majority. Quite soon afterwards, Madeleine and Lizzie inexplicably became fast friends, a strange turn of events. Whenever I questioned Maddy, she would blush slightly and then offer me some sort of assurance: "She is our half-sister." Or: "Lizzie has suffered cruelly these past few years. Can't you see how much she has changed?" Since I perceived nothing new in Lizzie's behaviour, I could not discover any basis upon which Maddy could have formed such an impression.

When I informed my sibling of my doubts, she would direct a vague smile in my direction, indicating, in its condescension, my inability to appreciate the radical shift of sensibility which had transformed our half-sister.

Then, Lizzie and Maddy suddenly announced they were to accompany Tom into London. I asked if I might accompany them. "Sister, your company would be much appreciated," Lizzie immediately responded, "but my oculist's reception room is almost too small for one, never mind four!" Not to be put off so easily, I claimed to have a number of errands of my own to accomplish. "Then, pray join us," Lizzie blithely rejoined.

On the drive into the City, my three companions remained resolutely silent. When I attempted to get some sort of response from Maddy on even the most mundane of matters, she simply answered yes or no or allowed the hint of a grimace to cross her face. The four of us disembarked at Regent Street, agreeing to meet in five hours' time at four o'clock.

I had lied. I had no errands to perform. I walked to no purpose that bright and radiant day. There was no warmth in my heart, so disturbed was I by the strange turn of events that was transpiring and which I felt helpless to control. I passed a wide assortment of establishments: watchmakers, butcher shops, slipper shops. Having turned down Charles Street from Oxford Street and gone through Soho Square into Greek Street, I came upon Mr. Wedgwood's magnificent establishment. I was astonished by the huge plate glass windows, through which his elaborate vases, urns, and dinner services could be seen glowing.

Even the wealthy merchants, I noticed, seemed to live above their shops — many sheds, obviously used as living quarters, leaned against the wall of houses made into shops.

I wandered further. I paid little attention to the other shoppers, some clad in great finery. Small dirty children, mainly boys, lurked at most corners and, at least twice, I witnessed one of these vagrants speeding down the street with a merchant in frenzied pursuit.

While strolling, I tried to puzzle out the situation which confronted me at Turnham Green. So frenzied was my attempt to puzzle out the situation that I wandered for a few hours, neglecting to drink a dish of tea or take any repast. Suddenly, I felt hot, a fever of some sort having gained possession of me. I halted. I noticed I was in front of a small terraced house. Desperately in need of water, I knocked at the portal. A few seconds later, a dusky-coloured boy — in looks very much like the urchins I had just seen during my promenade — answered. When I asked to see his mother, he pointed me in the direction of a small sofa directly opposite the door. I had only been seated a few moments when a side door opened and a woman, perhaps about five and forty and possessed of a dark complexion, came out to greet me. She was small, exceedingly compact, her figure bordering on the elegant. Dressed in quite ordinary fashion in red poplin, she soon impressed me with an almost radiant tranquillity.

"You have never been here before, Madam. What kind patron has sent you?"

Astonished, I replied that I had no idea what business was transacted in the house. I had simply stumbled upon her abode and being extraordinarily thirsty had knocked in order to beg a glass of water.

If she was taken aback, the woman did not show it. "Come into my receiving room and sit down," she instructed me. Then, her face became kind and gentle. "I'll fetch water."

The room to which I had been conducted was simple and small enough. A round table occupied the middle, the outskirts of the chamber being in the most neutral of decors. Strangely, no pictures of any kind graced the walls. Quite soon, the woman re-appeared, bearing a tumbler in her hand. She instructed me to sit at the table. When I had done so, she handed me the water and took her place opposite me. She then asked what circumstances had brought me to her home.

Not wishing to confide any of my fears to her, I simply told her that I had come into the city with some friends and was awaiting their return to the agreed meeting-spot at four.

"You have two hours before you. It would be best if you remain here."

"I should be an inconvenience."

"Not at all. My clients usually come only under the cover of darkness."

Startled by this admission, I summoned the bravery to inquire as to the nature of her profession.

"I am a fortune teller, specializing in the reading of the palm. I am known to many people of this city as Madame Salomé."

I tried not to show my disdain for such charlatanism. Surprisingly, this was not difficult to do because I was attracted to the remarkable serenity that accompanied all of this woman's movements. If she saw I was appalled, she did not betray her notice. Instead, she asked me why I, a person of my station, was wandering the streets?

At first, I was reserved, but the words soon rushed to escape my mouth. I had never liked Mortlake, I assured her, but, I went on, I was in touch with some deep uneasiness inhabiting my new home. I described Madeleine's strange behaviour in detail, becoming more and more overwhelmed by grief in the process. Suddenly, I burst into tears, uncontrollable sorrow having decisively escaped its boundaries.

Madame listened in attentive silence. There even seemed to be a warmth in the silence which enclosed her. She was not bothered by my tears, seemed almost welcoming of them. When I stopped the embarrassing stream of revelations, she remained silent for a long time, perhaps five minutes. Then she reached across the table, taking my hands in hers. "You have a remarkable sensitivity to the present. You do not possess the power to divine the future, however. You are seeing a chain of events which will take a sorry course. I cannot see more." Soon afterwards, I left Madame Salomé's to rejoin my companions a few streets away. My deep uneasiness continued unabated, but it was accompanied by a measure of consolation I took from the woman who had assisted me. Not one word was spoken on the return journey to Linden House.

On the 23rd — the very day of the above adventure — I supposedly appeared at the office of the Palladium Insurance Company, where, accompanied by Lizzie and Tom, I applied for my first life insurance policy. Two days later, the same party of three appeared at the Pelican, a day later at the Eagle. A number of policies were issued the following April.

part three
Eliza

Helen's account of life at Mortlake falsifies my early life. Unlike my half-sisters, I was an imaginative child, one who was curious, eager for knowledge. As you have gathered, Mrs. Abercromby — I too am loathe to call her Mother — was not a particularly indulgent parent, although a fervent practitioner of self-gratification. If you look carefully at Tom's crayon portrait of Helen, you will notice suspicious little pig eyes, snarling lips, and squirrel cheeks — features she inherited from Mrs. A. Not the most comely of women, but my parent — as I have already informed you — was a sensuous woman, a person who knew her way about in the carnal parts.

Me? I was fetching in a very subdued way. In addition to having inherited my mother's hair colouring, my tresses possessed a glorious natural curl. I was thin, never curvaceous. I dwelt on the edge of beautiful. That is what attracted men. They thought themselves essential to my completion. My suitors wanted to bestow *the* kiss which would fully awaken me. Women like me are more seductive than those with perfect beauty. I appealed to the artistic instincts lurking in the sex organs of most men.

My childhood and adolescence were not in any way remarkable. Mr. Ward, my father, was a womanizer. As you know, my mother became an adulterer. At a comparatively early age, I became bored. I went to dame school and developed into a voracious reader, although my options were severely limited. On principle, I dislike the word "romance" and never enjoyed the numerous confections in that genre written for ladies and promoted by the circulating libraries. I had to content myself with the likes of Jane Austen, whose strait-lacedness I could not abide. Nevertheless, I have a true literary imagination, one much more attuned to the characters in novels and the wretches who create them than to any person I have ever encountered in the flesh.

After Papa departed, Lieutenant A lived with Mother and me. Then, in short order, came Helen and Maddy. I never liked them. Born only ten months apart, they conducted themselves like twins forever swimming in the same amniotic fluid. They never needed me.

Although Maddy's features were more chiselled than Helen's, they looked alike. Sometimes a face is attractive or interesting even though there is not a single good feature in evidence. Everything converges in an interesting way. Maddy's eyes were a fraction larger than Helen's, her lips a bit smaller. *Some* people considered her beautiful, although no crayon drawing of her survives to prove this. *Most* people could not tell them apart.

Maddy was Helen's shadow, her emanation. Helen was the sun, Maddy the moon, forever satellite. Maddy did not have words until she was four. She didn't have to. In fact, I can't remember Helen ever using the first-person pronoun. Everything was "we" or "us." I felt excluded. I had no one:

my mother was an eager, early, and full-time proponent of the sexual rights of women, and the demon twins lived in the fetid air of a common bell jar.

Despite what Helen would have you believe, I was not a nymphet. I did, however, crave attention. I've already told you about that side of things. Up to my twentieth year, I had endured many sexual experiences, but I had not had a lover.

Tom's self-portrait does not reveal the remnants of a handsome face: it was much too narrow. His teeth were so crowded that his two front teeth protruded in rodent fashion, but he outfitted himself beautifully. Take my word for it, Tom was slightly more presentable when I met him in 1820. His hair had not yet begun to recede, he didn't always have his left eyebrow cocked at attention. He was a diminutive man (not significantly over five feet tall), but he was a rapacious lover, one very interested in "satisfying" his beloved.

I did not care about being satisfied. I did not love him. But it was difficult not to find him amusing. His narratives about his London adventures were intriguing. He was always filled with gossipy high spirits. My attention was never riveted on those self-satisfied bores, Hazlitt, De Quincey, or Charles Lamb (although, like me, the latter had a tension-filled home life in which he had to deal with a mad-dog sister).* No, my imagination fastened itself onto the tales of Tom's good friend, William Henry Ireland, who, employed as a lowly clerk in a law office, began to forge Shakespeare's signature on to a number of old records in his firm's vaults. Inspired by his father's love of the bard, he went on to write some new plays, extending the bard's canon and presumably his father's enjoyment. The old man,

---

*EDITOR'S NOTE: Like myself, Charles heard voices. In his twenties he was mentally deranged but, with the assistance of his dear sister, Mary, he recovered. In 1796, when she was thirty-two, Mary — herself subject to severe bouts of depression — murdered her mother in a fit of insanity. Despite these setbacks, brother and sister lived happily together and collaborated on the enchanting *Tales from Shakespeare,* my favourite book from childhood.

Samuel, was so convinced of the merits of these re-discovered masterpieces that he held an exhibition of the new manuscripts at his house on New Norfolk Street. A facsimile of the new plays, financed by papa, was published in 1795 but its authority was questioned by the pedant Edmund Malone. William promptly confessed his guilt.

As soon I heard this story, I wanted to meet William, who began his literary career anew (in 1815 his *Scribbleomania* was published) shortly after the dust from the Shakespeare fracas had settled. I wanted to know: had he uttered his forgeries because he adored his father and wanted to give him additional pleasure? Or had he despised his father and wanted to show the old dullard that he could not distinguish between a play written in 1585 and one composed in 1785? If that was his aim, he satisfied it. Or, had he been jealous of his father's love of the Bard (love misappropriated from himself) and sought to become "another" Shakespeare in order to win his father's affection? If that was an aim, he would never — unless caught — be able to have praise bestowed directly on him for his creativity. Or had William undertaken a ruse which he unconsciously knew would ultimately bring down shame on both himself and his father? The possibilities seemed endless.

I also listened attentively when Tom made verbal inventories of his Albany Street flat: a treasure trove of Bow and Chelsea shepherds and shepherdesses, Renaissance majolica, Sèvres bowls, Mughal paintings. Tom obviously had a good eye and knew where to look for things on the cheap. Soon, my mind was filled with a dazzling assortment of variously coloured baubles. I never doubted his word, but just in case I did Tom suddenly presented me one day with an exquisite cameo head of Flora, carved in high relief on a coral-coloured stone. The antiquary Richard Payne Knight had acquired this piece from the Italian dealer Angelo Bonelli for £100 in 1812. When Knight reached the brink of penury in 1815, Tom had gotten it for a song: a mere ten guineas. That gift was the declaration of love which put a seal on our pact to flee Mortlake.

London reached its apex of glory in 1820, the last year of
the Regency. There was Almack's Assembly Rooms in King
Street, where the ticket of admission promised entry into
the "seventh heaven of the fashionable world." All the men
had to wear knee breeches — even a man as great as the
Duke of Wellington was refused admission when he wore
only trousers.

There were bordellos catering to every persuasion.
There were puppet shows, freak shows, waxworks, shooting
galleries, taverns with skittle-alleys and bowling courts, bear
baitings, cockfights, masquerades, fêtes, and *ridottos*. On the
streets, you came upon all manner of spectacles: trained
mice, Nigger Minstrels, Punch and Judy men, performing
rabbits. If you went to Smithfield market, the ground was
covered, almost ankle-deep, in all manner of garbage; steam
rose from the reeking bodies of the cattle and then mixed
with the omnipresent fog in which the city was enveloped.
That place was filled with an unholy din, but there was
much to see: butchers, hawkers, barking dogs, pickpockets.

My own favourite form of entertainment was the same
as my husband's companion, Lord Byron: boxing. I once saw
the Jew, Daniel Mendoza, go for seventy-two rounds against
the "gentleman boxer" Richard Humphreys. I don't much
care for Jews, but I was glad to see the "gentleman" worsted.
For me, the more violent the match the better. In fact, I
adore violence, having learned through bitter experience
that this is usually the only way women can hope to
advance themselves.

At Stoke's Amphitheatre in the Islington Road women
often proved that they were just as proficient as men in this
kind of sport. I wrote this brief account of female gladiators,
which Tom published under his own name.

*Both women were very scantily clad, and wore little
bodices and very short petticoats of white linen. One of
these Amazons was a stout Irishwoman, strong and
lithe to look at, the other was a small Englishwoman,
full of fire and very agile. The first was decked with blue*

ribbons on the head, waist and right arm; the second wore red ribbons. Their weapons were a sort of two-handed sword, three or three and a half feet in length; the guard was covered, and the blade was about three inches wide and not sharp — only about half a foot of it was, but then that part cut like a razor. The spectators made numerous bets, and some peers who were there transacted some very large wagers. On either side of the two Amazons a man stood by, holding a long staff, ready to separate them should blood flow. After a time the combat became very animated, and was conducted with force and vigour with the broad side of the weapons. The Irishwoman presently received a great cut across her forehead, and that put a stop to the first part of the combat. The Englishwoman's backers (I amongst them) threw her shillings and half-crowns and applauded her. During this time the wounded woman's forehead was sewn up, this being done on stage; a plaster was applied to it, and she drank a good big glass of spirits to revive her courage, and the fight began again, each combatant holding a dagger in her left hand to ward off the blows. The Irishwoman was wounded a second time, and her adversary again received coins and plaudits from her admirers. The wound was sewed up, and the battle recommenced for the third time. The poor Irishwoman was destined to be the loser, for she now received a long and deep wound all across her neck and throat. The surgeon sewed it up, but she was too badly hurt to fight anymore. In any event, both combatants were dripping with perspiration, the Irishwoman bathed in blood. A few coins were thrown to console her: she died about two hours later.

I soon shared one of Tom's principal obsessions: gambling. Betting was one of the capital's greatest and most sustaining diversions. The metropolis burnt with that fever. One could bet on anything. Cricket, for example. This put a lot of pressure on the wicket-keepers, whose fingers often bled. At

Lord's, I once saw the wicket-keeper tear a fingernail off against his shoe buckle in picking up a ball. At White's (Tom's club), the members could bet on the duration of wars, the ages at which people would die, whether or not Mr. X would be able to sleep with his headachy wife on a particular night (Mr. X had to allow his wife's chambermaid's unbiased evidence — obtained by listening in at the keyhole — to settle this wager). One wet day, Lord A____ bet £3000 upon which of two raindrops would first reach the bottom of a window-pane.

Eating establishments often had gaming tables, two tables for loo, one for quinze, one for vingt-et-un, three or four for whist. The government tried to suppress gambling by allowing the press to publish details on the backroom dealings of establishments that did not conform to the Gambling Act of 1778: the names of the "operator" who dealt cards, of the "puffs" who were given money to play in order to decoy others to play, of the "clerks" who kept an eye on the "puffs," of the "dunners" who saw that losses were promptly paid up, of the "captains" who bounced anyone who complained too loudly of losing, of the "orderly men" who stood outside on the street and gave notice of the approach of the constables, and of the "runners" who paid the bribes to justices and like officials. According to government propaganda, gambling was immoral, but legal action was only taken against those "firms" which were unlicensed or did not pay bribes promptly enough.

So immersed were we in this world that Tom and I did not have time to marry until 1821, although one historian casts doubt on this by stating that no record of the ceremony exists (we were married on 14 June at Marylebone Register's Office). The same person also maintains that since I had no dowry beyond my beauty, I must have "manoeuvred him into matrimony with adroit subtlety."

The same wag also gives a rather precious account of our "lifestyle" at our new abode, 49 Great Marlborough Street, in the apartments once occupied by the fatuous Mrs. Siddons, the tragedienne. There, we supposedly began "entertaining with unstinted hospitality." We certainly gave suppers to which came the likes of John Clare, Thomas Hood, Allan Cunningham, H.F. Cary, Barry Cornwall, Sir David Wilkie, John Foster, and the greatest of all Lears, William Macready. At one party — unrecorded in any of the life records — William Blake in 1823 pinched my bottom.

Our financial resources fast dwindled. Tom contributed occasional articles to the *London Magazine* and painted what I can only term "dilettante" pictures, pale imitations of Morland and Stothard, artists then at the height of fashion. His combined earnings from these two pastimes, at a most sanguine estimate, can barely have totalled £100 a year. Half that figure would probably be nearer the mark. He did have £5000 in annuities left him by his grandfather, but this only gave us £250 per annum. He could hardly indulge his taste in costly books, engravings, china, and intaglios as extravagantly as he wanted to.

Our rooms in Great Marlborough Street were crammed with paintings, engravings, ceramics, sculptures, rare books, and manuscripts. When, by August 1821, we had eaten through £650 (my net profits from gambling were just over £300), I suggested we sell some things off. Tom was very reluctant to do this. He had bought these things at exceedingly low prices and wanted them to reach their full level of appreciation. Bailiffs started to call. Although I was bad tempered with them, they frightened me. No such persons had ever called at Mortlake on a daily basis. Tom did nothing.

In the midst of a heated discussion on the increasingly vexed issue of pecuniary insubstantiality, Tom mentioned that he had painted the occasional beggar by Rembrandt and one or two small Stubbses. I asked if he could do the same again. "That is a possibility, Madam," he assured me but then he allowed the matter to drop. A few days later, I broached the topic again. This time he was not so certain. Sales were down at both Sotheby's and Christie's, and the auctioneers, who had once turned a very blind eye to the items they took in for sale, had recently become slightly more inquisitive about provenance.

There were still many private collectors — those who bought from thieves — but they tended to ask "experts" to authenticate canvases presented for quick sale. The wealthy were still willing to be receivers of stolen goods, but they had to be the real thing. The fences had become the moral arbitrators of an item's authenticity. In short, thieves had become the consciences of other thieves. At this turning point, I became Tom's adept pupil in the art of imitation. But I joined this profession at precisely the wrong time, since the products of our atelier did not find buyers.

I must mention that Tom the collector was an ardent enemy of forgers. He always studied a painting, a piece of porcelain, or a carpet carefully before purchasing it. He took time to make diligent inquiries as to provenance. In fact, nothing made him angrier than the possibility of being taken in by a scoundrel selling something "inauthentic." The authorities, he averred, were too lenient in their prosecution of such offenders. Those vermin, he assured me one day, deserved transportation to the prison colony in Van Diemen's Land.

By the onset of 1822, Tom and I had few choices. We could discharge our servants, disengage ourselves from our busy rounds, and stay home together. We tried this for about a fortnight. Of course, it didn't work. One of Tom's friends, the pimply and ungainly Barry Cornwall (a very biased witness: he once propositioned me — I refused) made this observation about our domestic life: "Mrs. Wainewright was a sharp-eyed, self-possessed woman dressed in showy, flimsy finery. She seemed to obey Wainewright's humours, and to assist his needs; but much affection did not apparently exist between them."

"Flimsy" is one of those notions which exist only in the eye of the beholder. I didn't wear see-through clothes, and my dresses were of the finest cloth. I agree I was "sharp-eyed" (I've had to be), but I never "obeyed" Tom. Once upon a time, I liked him; now, financial misery made me loathe Tom's company. I couldn't remain cooped up with him. I made a suggestion, which Tom was very eager to follow. If he was so expert at forgery and passing off the resulting goods, would it not be possible to forge his trustees' signatures on his own annuities and thus liberate us from our present embarrassment?

Three trustees stood in Tom's way: his uncle Robert and his two cousins, Edward Smith Foss and Edward Foss (father and son). The younger Foss, who had been at school with Tom at Greenwich, considered himself a bit of a connoisseur: he wrote for the *London Magazine*, the *Athenaeum*, the *Gentleman's Magazine*, and such like. Tom was loathe to deceive these men, particularly since he and Foss junior were members of the same club, where they often took lunch together. But, I reminded Tom, a man who has forged Rembrandts can surely contrive to reproduce three signatures and, in the process, use his considerable charm so as not to arouse the suspicions of the minor bureaucrats with whom he would be in contact.

On 15 July 1822, Tom presented himself at the Bank of England with a notarized power of attorney converting the £5000 to £5250 in a riskier, but higher paying annuity. The clerks with whom Tom dealt were not even mildly suspicious. So ten days later, Tom, having acquired a working knowledge of the Bank's procedures, presented himself to the same officials with a new power of attorney, this one allowing him £2250 in cash proceeds. Two years later, on 17 May 1824, Tom withdrew the remaining £3000. During the intervening two year period, no official of the Bank contacted any of the Trustees.

It is one thing to rob one's own coffer, but it is another to have nothing left in the coffer. Unfortunately, the two incursions into the forbidden funds purchased us only short-term relief. I had been certain that I would be able, through my remarkable success as a gamester, to recoup the money and repay the borrowed funds. At first, my luck held out. I increased the initial withdrawal of £2250 to just over five thousand guineas within a month and I would have been able to hold the line between extravagance and the bailiffs if I had been able to curb Tom's lascivious eye, which went on more and more frequent shopping sprees. By the middle of 1823 we were down to just over three hundred pounds. We survived (just) through the spring of 1824, but then we were inundated once again with creditors and their bailiffs.

The second infusion of funds was exhausted by the middle of 1827. Once again we hobbled along, making ends not meet. There were further complications. I was, after six years of marriage, pregnant. I was not overjoyed. One journalist — citing the rejected Barry Cornwall as his source — records the matter with the usual grace and tact of his profession: "He noted that the child, born to Mrs. Wainewright in 1828, was '(scandal whispered) the son of a dissipated and impoverished peer.'" You will notice that this is gossip within gossip within gossip. The child was Tom's. Adultery cannot be added to the list of my failings.

There was one further change in my life about which I must now acquaint you. For some time, I had had to put up with the company of Neptune, my husband's Newfoundland (while Tom was at Mortlake he had been boarded with William Ireland). When I was with child and could not leave our rooms on Great Marlborough Street, the beast began to annoy me more and more. He craved attention, was friendly in an overly enthusiastic fashion. He almost pushed me over a few times, so eager was he to share the joys of his doggy heart with me. He had a nature too easily pleased. I informed Tom that the animal would have to leave or be destroyed.

Tom was aghast. He would not heed my plea. I wanted to be alone, the dog followed me everywhere. Finally, I resorted to strychnine, the bitter alkaloid of a tree (*Strychnos nux-vomica*) native to Ceylon, India, and the antipodes. We had used this drug on rats at Mortlake, but Neptune could be a fussy eater. Unlike the rodents I was accustomed to, he sniffed at the meals composed of three parts meat to one part drug. Finally, I gave him severely reduced rations for two days and, on the morning of the third, mixed the alkaloid with chicken broth. The convulsions began about an hour later and he died four

hours after their onset. With a few tears trickling down my
cheeks, I broke the news of Neptune's end and put the
blame on our wealthy neighbours' manservant, who had
been attempting to control a rat infestation.

From that experience, I learned some lessons. First, a
simple poison — as opposed to a glamorous, elusive
concoction — is the treatment of choice. Its effects are
well-documented and remarkably effective. Second, many
persons have ready access to the major poisons. It is difficult
to pin down a malefactor if many individuals have or could
purchase that drug. Third, even the noxious taste and odour
of strychnine can be disguised by a good thick broth or a
heavy cream sauce.

My newly acquired interest in poison was not of any
help in resolving our financial problems. We had exhausted
the money in annuities. I could no longer move comfortably
about and attend at the gambling houses. Having nowhere
to turn, we accepted an invitation from Tom's uncle to live
at Linden House, to where we moved in September 1827. I
was bereft: Linden House may have been tantalizingly close
to London but at that time it was a half-day's trek.

For some, Linden House was a beautiful oasis of
Georgian refinement. Everything was so controlled: the
spartan interiors of the rooms, the rigorous beauty of the
facade (in my opinion, too much Palladianism can be a
disaster), and the severely straight lines of the vistas in the
garden. A true palace of rationalism, lacking any semblance
of a heart.

George Edward Griffiths was the kind of man to whom
some women instinctively — and condescendingly — refer
as a "pet." He was kind, sweet, and very dull. Almost totally
bald, this twig of a man dressed in a suit and wig of the late
eighteenth century, almost as if he had never quite left the
century of his birth. Very much a gentleman of the old
school, he carried himself as well as he could despite his
scoliosis, shuffled quietly into rooms, and took snuff in an
unostentatious fashion. His father had evidently been a man
of enormous energy and drive, but Uncle seemed drained of

ambition. Perhaps Tom — in his typically perverted way — had inherited his grandfather's soaring spirits.

My uncle-in-law was punctilious in asking about my condition and instructing his housekeeper, Sarah Handcocks, to give me a glass of port after every meal. He had published several gynaecological treatises which proffered this recommendation, and he was certain it was sound advice. Mr. Griffiths was nervous around Tom, although he obviously loved him. He did not understand Tom, although he would have liked to.

Life at Linden House was insufferably boring. As my confinement drew nigh, I noticed that Tom was becoming more and more attached to his uncle. I suspected the worst: Tom's new-found bond might become even stronger after our child was born. If this happened, I might have to sacrifice the pleasures of London for cozy family evenings in the country. I had to be decisive.

On the morning of 5 February 1828, I summoned my husband to my bedroom and instructed him: "Tonight, *boeuf en danube* will be served. You are to eat none of the portion offered you. You will claim to have a headache or state that your stomach is indisposed."

"Madam, what is transpiring?"

"Sir, ask me no questions and it will be for the best for both of us."

He was about to offer, in his exceedingly tedious way, some rejoinder, but, with a short wave, I dismissed him. He advanced towards the door, paused for a few seconds, and departed.

That evening, after the first two courses, I claimed to be ill and asked for water. Mrs. Handcocks, who took her meals with us, got up to fetch it. As soon as she left the room, I claimed that I could not wait and followed her directly into the kitchen. After she handed me the tumbler of water, I told her that I was faint and would rest a moment. I instructed her to see after Mr. Griffiths and Mr. Wainewright. Cook, the only other person then in the room, went about her business. As soon as I was certain of not being observed, I removed the poison, secreted in a tiny packet on my person, and dropped it into the main course. Then, I returned to the dining room.

I was taking a calculated risk. Mrs. H usually did not partake of the main course. Unlike Mr. Griffiths, a sliver of a man with a lustful appetite, she was a large woman who consumed little food. When the serving maid entered the room with the main course, she served Mr. Griffiths, then Tom, then me, then Mrs. H. Everything went as usual, but I became frightened when Mrs. H did not signal the maid to skip her. She even looked at the concoction with — what seemed to me — considerable fascination. Since I could not have two people die, I was on the verge of pretending to another fit of faint.

But I didn't have to do anything. When Mrs. H noticed that Tom was not eating, she began to cross-question him on his health. Tom shrugged his shoulders, mentioning that he was in need of a good tonic. Mrs. H began to ramble on about the various potions known to her and, in the midst of these reflections, seemed to lose all interest in her meal. Meanwhile, Mr. Griffiths ate his portion with his customary gusto. Only then did he turn to his housekeeper of twenty-four years to point out that this evening's repast was not up to Cook's high standards.

"What can the matter be, sir?" a startled Mrs. H inquired. She was surprised because Mr. Griffiths never uttered a complaint about anything.

"The broth is exceedingly bitter."

Mrs. H immediately rose from the table and made for the kitchen. Before she had even reached the passage door, her employer fell to the floor. He screamed in anguish, claiming that he could feel knives carving out his stomach from the inside. Mrs. H ran off to find a footman, who could be dispatched for a doctor. Meanwhile, the servants were in a flurry. I ordered them to compose themselves and to remove all plates from the table. This they did quickly. As soon as this task was accomplished, I re-entered the kitchen and ordered the entire crew to their quarters, where they were to offer a communal prayer for the health of their employer. As soon as they left, I disposed of all remnants of the *boeuf* on the serving platter and in Cook's pot.

Mr. Griffiths died four hours later. If the physician who attended him had any inclination to investigate the origin of his patient's sudden demise, those reflections were broken by his having to attend me, for I had gone into labour. Obviously, the sheer moments of torture I had suffered at the hands of Mrs. H had unnerved me. I gave life to my son less than an hour after the death of Tom's uncle. Tom, who had indeed grown increasingly fond of his uncle, insisted on calling the boy Griffiths. Given the remarkable circumstances of my child's birth, I could hardly refuse.

My triumph in ridding Tom of his uncle was short-lived. The circulation of *The Monthly Review* had dwindled under George Edward's charge, and, what is more, he had dissipated his father's wealth. Tom was left a mere £5000 and Linden House, which cost over a thousand pounds a year to maintain in minimal fashion. We had debts of over £10,000. In some ways, we were now in a worse predicament and had a new mouth demanding to be fed.

To my surprise, Tom was not particularly put out by this turn in circumstance. Always a patriarch, Tom now fancied himself as lord of the manor, complete with son and heir. I was furious. We were stuck at Linden House with a child that demanded constant attention; we were encumbered with massive loans; we had no ready money. We were compelled to pay over four thousand pounds to those persons who threatened to burn Linden House to the ground if obligations to them were not met. An oblivious Tom bought yet more pieces of bric à brac and allowed the grasping merchants of Turnham Green the privilege of supplying him with goods on credit.

Within a year, we were reduced to a new level of destitution, even though we were ensconced in a magnificent country estate. I felt helpless and had nowhere to turn. Then, a gleam of light. In February 1829 Tom heard from Edward Foss junior, who had been to Mortlake in connection with the settlement of an estate, that Mrs. Abercromby and the two girls were on the verge of selling up. Apparently, a loan taken by my mother had been called in. Edward told Tom that the situation was not as bad as it seemed: Mrs. A would have over £100 in ready cash from the sale, the contents of the house, and the title of the other properties she rented out.

I was also aware that my mother might be inclined to bestow her entire estate upon me. Unlike Helen and Maddy, I did not have a life income from army pensions granted on fraudulent pretenses. The amount in question was indeed minute: perhaps a maximum of five hundred pounds, but it would buy us a little time. In November 1829 I invited Mother and the girls to live with us at Linden House, an invitation which was accepted with alacrity, although the three of them did not arrive until 5 March 1830.

Matricide is not a deed to which even someone with my steely constitution can turn to without a great deal of trepidation. My hesitations vanished when the three Abercrombys arrived at Linden House. In the ten years since I had laid eyes on her, my mother had become even more grossly fat and, in keeping with her appearance, more loud and vulgar. She showed little interest in my offspring Griffiths, a handsome toddler of just over two. Mrs. A's chief interest in life was now in eating, and she announced her intention of taking full advantage of any culinary delicacies that Cook and her staff might have to offer.

My half-sisters had not changed much. Even I now found it difficult to tell the wenches apart, although, as I indicated earlier, Maddy had slightly finer features than Helen. As before, Helen still did all the talking for the two of them. I could not but think back to years before, at how Helen's plain speaking concealed a tormented heart — when she found it necessary to her own selfish ends, she had done away with that little wretch, Theo. In any event, the two dull little girls had become sullen women with, as before, not much to say for themselves.

I had to study the situation unfolding before me. Prudently, I decided to wait two or three months before serving mother her final meal. Then, to my considerable astonishment, I noticed, a few days after the group's arrival, that Maddy's appearance had taken on a new life. Her cheeks glowed, her eyes gleamed, and her skin had a radiance previously absent. She no longer accompanied Helen everywhere.

My woman's intuition told me that Maddy was in love — but with whom? Then, at supper that evening, I noticed the furtive glances Maddy directed at my husband. My youngest sister was like a prisoner who, deprived of light for years, falls in love with the first sun-drenched object she beholds. I cannot think of any other explanation for this sudden infatuation.

That evening, I took Tom aside. Had he noticed how Maddy's eyes were riveted on him? He claimed to be completely unaware of the young woman's interest. I instructed him to pursue the matter to its logical conclusion. Two days later, he proudly informed me that he had "lanced" her the night before. He added some inconsequential details: in that having had his way with her, he had seized her maidenhead and that she was a "ravenous" partner. "You are a perfect match for each other," I reflected to myself. How far, I wondered, would Maddy go in pursuit of Tom? How much did she want him?

I told Tom that I intended to enforce my conjugal rights to sole possession of his body. Therefore, he was to inform Maddy that I had discovered what was afoot and wanted all intercourse between them to cease. At table that evening, I was pleased to see the look of complete devastation which criss-crossed her face. Later that evening, I spoke to her privately in order to list my requirements for an accommodation.

I began by telling her that I was aware that she had slept with my husband, but, I assured her, I had no wish to

123

inform either Mother or Helen of what had transpired. However, Tom was my property, and I would relinquish him only if certain prerequisites were met. Maddy asked for an enumeration.

Such conditions, I assured her, would be mutually beneficial but might be deeply upsetting to Mother and Helen. Only if she was determined to have Tom could I declare myself openly. I advised her to consider the matter fully.

While Mother and Helen strolled in the garden next day, Maddy approached me: "Sister, tell me your requirements. I shall fulfil them." In the few days which had followed my amazing discovery, I had been able to give my imagination full scope. The plan was simple but had many complex interlocking parts which had to be woven together, *viz.*

1. Maddy, masquerading as Helen, would accompany Tom and me to London, where we would take out a large number of insurance policies on Helen's life, payable to herself and Tom.

2. Mother was, before the end of the year, to die.

3. The acquisition by such a young, obviously healthy woman of a number of life insurance policies would hopefully arouse a great deal of suspicion on the part of those firms that a plot was afoot to murder her. (My instincts as a gambler informed me that most of the firms in question would issue policies with the expectation that if Helen were murdered or died under mysterious circumstances, they would not pay up.)

4. Within a year, Helen would die. As soon as the investigation of her mysterious passing was underway, I would flee to France and, in the process, attract the retribution of the law. Tom would declare his innocence, and Maddy would support those claims.

5. Tom and Maddy would collect the proceeds from the various policies and would, subsequently, convey half of the resultant amount to me in exile. If they failed to do so, I would expose them.

If she was shocked, Maddy did not appear so. I knew that she did not like or love Mrs. A, but I thought that she might balk at disposing of Helen. She simply said: "She has thick ankles." However, Maddy wanted to be assured that the plan was foolproof. I recounted the sudden ends of Neptune and Mr. Griffiths. For the very first time in her short life, she seemed to realize that all is fair in infatuation and war.

Maddy's obsession with Tom had obviously opened up a world of glorious possibilities. First, I might be able to start my life all over again. Second, I looked forward to matching my wits and limited resources against the insurance firms. For a woman who had discovered comparatively late in life that she was a born gambler, this was a splendid opportunity to win against all the odds.

On 22 March, a few days after sealing our pact, Maddy, Helen, Tom, and I journeyed to London, leaving Mother behind. Helen departed soon after we arrived; then, I took the opportunity to coach Maddy in exactly what she was to say when and if the actuaries inquired why she, such a young, healthy woman, wanted to take out policies on her life. The answer was straightforward: she was an heiress who would come into her estate within three years; before she did so, she wanted to insure that members of her family (i.e., her mother, brother-in-law, and particularly her sister, Madeleine) were protected lest her death — although an unlikely one — were to deny them their great expectations.

When, after a number of inconvenient and expensive visits to London and the expenditure of over £80 cash in insurance premiums, we arrived triumphantly home on the 1st of May, we discovered a sheriff's officer installed in our house. The merchants of Turnham Green had issued warrants against us. Tom and I did our best to withstand this new assault on our freedom but on 8 July we were obliged to grant a bill of sale on the entire furniture and effects of Linden House. The chief culprit was the appropriately named Mr. Sharpus, a crockery merchant who ran a money-lending business on the quiet. To the same person Tom was also indebted, under an attorney's warrant, for £610, which was to fall due in August. Through cumbersome negotiations with that lawyer, we reached an agreement that the warrant and bill should be held over until 21 December.

Needless to say, my mother became extremely upset by this calamity. She was desperately worried that, having been turned out of one home, she was about to be cast asunder from her new one. I assured her that everything would work out for the best. Of course, I used this conversation to discover the state of her finances. She had a personal estate of £1500 plus some real estate in Mortlake. Since my sisters held army pensions, she offered to make over all her assets to me. The will was notarized on 13 August.

My mother died six days later. I had become so adept at this sort of thing that it seems almost pointless to recall the circumstances of her passing. The dish this time was lobster thermidor. Mrs. H was away visiting with her brother in Edgware, and Helen was not at table. Maddy told me that Helen's menses occurred very regularly and that she always took to her bed on the first day of its onset. Maddy timetabled the event precisely and everything was thus in order for Mother's leave-taking. When the poison hit her system, she scanned all the faces in the room, looking for all the world like a demented Lady Macbeth, who realizes that the knife has finally been stuck where it belongs — in her own back. She collapsed to the floor, her rolls of fat cushioning the silent fall.

The next three months were dreadful. Tom, Maddy, and I that autumn renewed in earnest our assault upon the insurance companies. The sum total of monies due to us upon Helen's death was £12,000, but our outlay was considerable: £220. As Christmas approached, we were desperately short of ready money and the baker, grocer, butcher, and coal merchant refused to provide us with any goods or services. On Sunday 12 December, we left Linden House to the sole occupation of the bailiff. Our very sad party of seven (Tom, Griffiths, my two sisters, Sarah Handcocks, another old retainer, Harriet Grattan, and myself) made its way to furnished lodgings at 12 Conduit Street over the shop of a tailor called Nicoll. This three-bay stuccoed building was embellished with giant Ionic pilasters and pedimented first-floor windows. Outwardly magnificent, our accommodation therein was shabby. We had suddenly become impoverished gentility, members of an undesirable social strata.

On the following day, in search of diversion, we saw our old friend Macready perform at Drury Lane in *The Stranger*. After the play, we returned to Conduit Street, where we consumed a meal of ale and lobsters. The next night, we again attended at Drury Lane, this time we saw *The School for Scandal*, although Tom had expressed a preference for the Royal Surrey, where the second piece on the bill was an entertainment called *Van Diemen's Land*. Before we set out that night, I warned Tom and Maddy that they were not to consume anything from the after-theatre supper which would be awaiting us upon our arrival back on Conduit Street.

On our walk back to our lodgings, the streets were damp from a recent shower. Helen complained that her feet were wet and retired to change her shoes and stockings. She returned to say that she had caught a chill and did not feel like partaking of our meal. I insisted that she have a bit of the oysters and bottled porter. She refused, but Maddy seemed to be pleading with her to stay. Finally, she sat down. Maddy looked in turn at me and at Tom. Then, directing her gaze across the table at Helen, she commanded her: "Do not eat any of this food." After she made this declaration, Maddy calmly and with great relish tucked into the oysters. She died a week later.

part four

The Voices

[EDITOR'S NOTE: In the interests of accuracy, I must state that the following messages were dictated to me at various times during the nine months in which I received the communications. Unlike the longer pronouncements which were received sequentially, these statements were promulgated higgledy-piggledy. Rather than interrupt the flow of the narrative, I have decided to insert them here, at the instigation and advice of my learned husband, as a sort of entr'acte.]

SARAH WALSH

Amazed! Flabbergasted! These are the only words that come to mind when I hear of Tom's adventures. He was always a creature bordering on wildness. He had to be curbed *leniently*. I never dared to speak to the old

Master on this score, but I was direct with Mr. Griffiths junior on many occasions. I urged him to make much of the boy. He looked at me uncomprehendingly, as if I were speaking in a foreign tongue. He would smile pleasantly enough in my direction and then would wander out of the room. Not high-and-mighty like his father, he listened and then fled.

The child had a cruel streak in him, some would say vicious. But he was a tiny lad without mother or father. I would not want you to think his grandfather a cruel man. Perhaps strait-minded as well as strait-jacketed. I am sure he consumed those paper boxes as some sort of practical joke.

To tell the truth, I thought the child took after his grandfather. He certainly looked a great deal like him. I always thought the child revered Mr. Griffiths Senior. The old man had adored his daughter, had been torn apart when she died. He didn't want to carry a grudge — perhaps he could not escape the burden of one. As for Tom, he was more harsh on himself than he ever was on others. A deprived child — they are always more sinned against than sinning.

SOPHIA ABERCROMBY

Pish! Tosh! My daughters — all three of them — were preposterous little witches, never satisfied with anything I tried to do for them. Permit me to apologize on their behalf. So blackened have they my character I'm not sure you will want to hear my side of things. You probably think I don't have a side worth defending.

My fortunes took a sharp dip after the deaths of my two husbands. I had to manage money carefully and precisely. I was not promiscuous. I strived to keep my ahead above water financially and — for my trouble — I was murdered.

From earliest childhood, Eliza, her brow tightly furrowed and her fierce eyes burrowing into you, was a child unresponsive to any display of affection; Helen was as cold as any cod snatched from the deepest waters of the ocean. Only Madeleine was in the least bit responsive to a mother's love.

As for Tom. A very well-made little dabble of a man. But the nonsense that spouted forth from the large mouth of this miniature being! Not to be countenanced!

SARAH HANDCOCKS

Tom Wainewright was a mingy excuse for a human being, always tardy in paying wages. Mrs. W! She was even worse. A stingy so-and-so who piled my back up with chore after chore. Her poor sister — Miss Madeleine I thought she was — never recovered from the passing over of Miss Helen. She was a gentle creature — not warm but friendly. Would sometimes give me a hand with the chores, saying she needed to do something to distract herself.

RALPH GRIFFITHS

The child Tom was a sneak, wastrel, a complete good-for-nothing. He never listened to any instruction with which I favoured him. I judged him an infernal little sneak, not worth the time of a decent man. He needed to be brought to account frequently and sharply. He was a consummate liar, a forger, a poisoner, fully deserving of the ignominy surrounding his wretched surname. He had no understanding of the pleasure of practical jokes.

GEORGE GRIFFITHS

The child Tom had a gentle aspect to him. He could invent all manner of stories; his copies of some of the paintings at Linden House were remarkably dexterous. Remarkably like my sister in his nature: enthusiastic but unfixed and undisciplined. I never understood why Father could never detect the similarity between mother and son. Acorns never falling far, etc. Yet, the old man disliked the boy unduly. For me, the boy had a surfeit of feeling. Not a good quality in anyone.

Mrs. W was a creature of the most exquisite proportions and manners. Since I really didn't want to live, I cannot be too angry with her.

WILDE

I suffered so much in the latter part of my life that I cannot bear to throw any more stones in any man's direction, much less Thomas Wainewright's.

JOHN SCOTT

Wainewright was a man of incredible cleverness, although deeply superficial. He refused all guidance, being a man of immoderate conceit. I know him to be an insidious liar: my death took place in Covent Garden. If placed in an exhibition case devoted to beautiful insects, Tom is a brilliantly coloured Admiral butterfly, the thorax thoroughly excavated.

FUSELI

If you will permit, the correct spelling is Füssli. I take the opportunity to mention my irritation at those art historians who accuse me of being a mere fetishist, the hairdos of my female subjects supposedly constructed of pudendal hair. So foolish, to confuse a stylistic trademark with a perversion. Typical of the ways in which envious art historian hacks attack those who provide them with bread and butter. Unlike Tom, I was not a counterfeiter. He was an exceedingly ingenious fellow.

BLAKE

My lot — even in eternity — lies in opposition. Tom had the pride of the peacock. What higher compliment can I pay him?

BYRON

The great — such is their eminence! — deserved or not — are always at the service of the rabble — not content with making their causes at one with the sentiments of the fine intellects of this world — must vilify them with consummate lies! Wainewright — blackguard!

MADELEINE

— *I am the space that was abandoned, the non-murdered. Certainly a victim.*
— *I am the person who took her own life. A victim at my own hands.*
— *I am the woman who never really was. Definitely a victim.*
— *I am anonymous. I am one of those who, given no choices, are liberated from apologies. Nevertheless, a victim.*

This is my credo. My former life — such as it was — washes over me, even now filling me with anxiety in my tranquil spirit world. Strange feelings for a woman who allowed others to write her scripts for her. Nevertheless, from earliest childhood, I became the text others inscribed. Mother was harsh *and* abrasive. Eliza was scheming *and* self-serving. Helen was protective *and* self-centred. Tom was charming *but* spineless. Such a strange assortment of persons to be the only spokes on the wheel of my short span on this earth.

133

Their voices are even more outlandish. From earliest childhood: "Madeleine, you must learn to do exactly what you are told." *Then*: "Madeleine, you are insufferably stupid." *Then*: "Maddy, you are the centre of my life. Follow my lead." *Then*: "Maddy, I adore you. You must help me."

If I tell you I was gentle, you will think me insipid. If I tell you I paid no heed to insults, you will label me stupid. If I tell you I often enjoyed Helen's company, you will consider me dull. If I tell you I was touched by Tom's attentions, you will judge me flattery's victim.

Deprived of an imagination, I lack tropes, images, symbols. Mine is almost an eternal silence. If you ignore me, you are in good company.

part five

Helen

I shall have a great deal to say — especially about the veracity of Lizzie's account — but before I can do so, we must return to that post-theatre supper on 14 December 1830. After issuing her injunction to me, Maddy continued to eat for a few moments and then burst into a fit of uncontrollable laughter: "Sister, you know that oysters have never agreed with you. Have a bit of the porter." She was correct about oysters, but, for form's sake, I would have eaten a bit of the meagre repast. Neither Lizzie nor Tom touched their food. They exchanged puzzled looks and then Lizzie called in the direction of the kitchen for Mrs. Gratton to remove the plates and serving dishes.

By this time, Maddy's merriment had ceased. Slowly, she pushed herself away from the table, rose and left the room. In the middle of the night, she became violently ill. The next

morning, she claimed to have a bad cold. Tom sent out to a
chemist for a remedy — a black dose — which she took.*
When she did not noticeably improve, I insisted that a
doctor be called.

Immediately, Lizzie summoned me to her chamber,
where she imparted most of the information she has given
you. In particular, she outlined Maddy's involvement with
the insurance companies and mother's gruesome death.
Maddy had taken poison intended for me and, except for
her strong constitution, should have been dead. Deeply
frightened by her reversal of fortune, Lizzie promised me
that she would do what she could to save Maddy's life, but
she warned me of the consequences attendant on my non-
cooperation. As far as Lizzie was concerned, she was
summoning a physician to examine "Helen Abercromby." If
I said a word which contravened this deceit, she would
expose Maddy as an accessory to the murder of her own
mother. Not only were my lips to be sealed, I was now to
answer to the name of Maddy. At first, I was convinced that
the fraud would be readily evident, but Mrs. Gratton and
Mrs. Handcocks were old, nearly blind, and hard of hearing;
Griffiths spoke only a handful of words. Of course, Maddy
and I were not known to anyone else in London.

On the following day, Dr. Locock of Hanover Square
was called in. Austere and officious, he had no semblance of
a bedside manner. His testimony survives: "I found her
sitting in her bedroom, complaining of a great headache, a
weight over her eyes, and partial blindness. She had a full,
labouring pulse, and shooting pains about the head." He
prescribed alternate draughts of calomel and senna as
aperients. On the next day, when her condition had not
improved, he recommended that she be bled with a cupping
glass. He told Lizzie that he had never seen a patient change

---

*EDITOR'S NOTE: Helen is the only one of the spirits who frightens me. She is so
fierce, so self-righteous in her hatreds. I am loathe to provide any kind of
supplement to her utterances in the event she takes offence. However, I must
point out that this concoction was sometimes called the "black drop" — a
mixture of opium, vinegar, and assorted spices.

so much in appearance in such a short period of time: earlier, he had examined "Helen" on behalf of one of the insurance firms.

That afternoon, "Helen" turned feverish. Sarah, Harriet, and I were in constant attendance, although Lizzie was always close at hand. On Saturday, the patient's pulse remained febrile. Locock ordered a tartar emetic, which led to renewed vomiting. By Sunday, she had recovered a bit of her eyesight and was allowed chicken broth. That night, she was restless and hysterical. On the next day, camphor was prescribed.

On Tuesday, the patient had been extremely ill for a week. Locock asked Lizzie to insure that Griffiths was kept under control so that his patient was not placed under additional stress. "Helen" was well enough to ask if she could eat some meat. Locock agreed to this and a request for a cup of coffee.

Just after noon, Lizzie, Tom, and Griffiths went out for a walk. At the door, Lizzie asked me to add the camphor jelly powder to the coffee. About half an hour later, the patient was delirious, imagined a little boy coming into the room, and that he had no business there. Harriet and I tried to settle "Helen" and immediately sent messages summoning a doctor and an apothecary. Pedantic and bumbling Edward Hanks, one of the assistants at King and Nicholson's, was attending the patient when a very annoyed Dr. Locock arrived. He later stated: "She was in convulsions resembling those which were the effect of a wound, and was hysterical."

The patient cried out: "Oh, doctor, I am dying; I feel I am — I am sure so." The doctor blandly assured her that this was not so: "You'll get better by and by." The doctor further vented his annoyance at the presence of the chemist by ordering Hanks to use a different medicine. Suddenly, "Helen" became calm: "Doctor, I was gone to hell, but you have brought me back to earth!" Then, Harriet burst out: "Miss Helen is dying of the same evil that carried off her mother!" Locock told her to keep

137

quiet, but the patient warmly responded: "Yes, my poor mother — oh, my poor mother." As soon as his patient was settled, Locock took his leave.

Then, an eerie stillness enveloped Maddy. I left the room. When I returned, another fit of convulsions came on. I sent for Dr. Locock, who arrived at precisely four o'clock. When we reached her bedroom, Maddy was dead, one hand tightly grasping the wrist of Mrs. Gratton. Lizzie, Tom, and Griffiths arrived just as Locock took his final leave on that sad day. Tom inquired the cause of his sister-in-law's death. The physician told him: "Mischief in the brain."

My sister was less than twenty years old when she abandoned this exceedingly sad vale of tears. She was a poor, unassuming girl, whom two fiends used for their own evil purposes. I must give credence to this, since I never had the opportunity to speak privately with my sister in her final, long week of agony. I am certain that Lizzie has lied grievously in her account when she describes Maddy's motivation in assisting her wicked designs. Lizzie may have threatened to kill me if she resisted her. Why else would she have swallowed the poison? Maddy was too much attached to me, and it is I who am guilty if those feelings led her to rebel against me. I remain convinced her suicide was motivated by the desire to protect me. I am sure I inadvertently administered the last lethal dose of strychnine. Locock later testified that he never prescribed a powder of any kind, and Hanks stated that the camphor was in the form of pills.

There is another gruesome irony at work. It would be impossible for two brothers to switch identifies as easily as Maddy and I did. We looked and spoke alike, had no real identities under law, and so, in a crucial moment, could become body substitutes. So I now was thrust into the role of unwitting accomplice to Lizzie and Tom. For the remainder of my life my real name was taken from me. I became Madeleine.

On the day of "Helen's" death, Locock and Hanks

returned to Conduit Street, where they opened up the head of the corpse. During that examination, they discovered a considerable quantity of water on the lower part of the brain, pressing upon the upper part of the spinal marrow. The ventricles of the brain were overfilled, as well as the blood vessels servicing the brain. The surgeon and apothecary reached an accord: oysters and wet feet had infected the blood vessels more than was common. There was, they agreed, nothing in the state of the stomach to cause a suspicion of foul play.

So on a cold, wet, and foggy 23rd of December — two days before Christmas — I attended my own burial at Bunhill Fields, the resting spot for Dissenters and the impoverished. The service was conducted by a grizzled old priest, who raced through the words which were supposed to bestow consolation and re-assurance. On leaving the cemetery, I strolled away from Tom and Lizzie. On my long walk back to Conduit Street, I was at first hemmed in by dark figures who wove around and behind me on the streets. My sister was now a spirit, but I lived in a world of ghosts.

Deeply frightened both by my sister's death and by the prospect of having to live with her murderers, I thought of making my way to Madame Salomé's. I rejected that notion, so well had I schooled myself in not sharing sorrow. Suddenly the streets were filled. Perhaps I had not been paying attention. Now it had become a typical London day: children defying parents, the poor searching for some bread to buy at a price within reach, street vendors with all manner of sweets and sugar drinks, gin-soaked beggars plunked down in front of the emporia catering to the wealthy. Then, finally, the fog settled in, making it almost impossible to see more than two feet ahead. That miasma provided the perfect accompaniment to my despair.

By the time I neared our lodgings, it was dinner time, and the crowd had thinned out. Then, I saw a solitary figure — male — who lurked at a corner. As I advanced towards this pitiful creature costumed in oily rags, I could not help but notice how bone-thin he was. Then I beheld the face of the servant boy, Theo, now a man of twenty years or thereabouts, staring out at me from that miserable little body. The smile — both eager and open — was the same. Even further reduced in wretchedness since childhood, his countenance still bore a look of unrequited cheerfulness. I am not certain he recognized me. I continued on my way.

I did not wish to rest under the same roof as the Wainewrights, but I had no choice. The old serving women, who had stayed behind with Griffiths, put up a pretence of cheerfulness, but I knew that, like me, they had no one to whom they could apply for assistance. "Was the service a comfort, Maddy?" Mrs. Gratton inquired.

At Bunhill Fields, there are a few mausoleums. During the internment, I looked at these structures and pondered what it would be like to be shut up in one of them. I did not have to wait very long to find out. My room, which I had shared with Maddy, was exceedingly small, as were all the other chambers we rented. The sounds of agitation made by my little nephew, who was thoroughly confused by the strange disappearance of one of his aunts, filled them. Tom, always a highly nervous person, was even more out of his skin than customary. Lizzie had become quieter. I feared her silence.

That Christmas was the most awful I have ever endured. Lizzie spent the day in bed, and Tom was away for most of the day. The two old women and I entertained Griffiths. Tom seemed strangely elated, as if he were cautiously optimistic that his fortunes had picked up. I think Tom thought that the insurance companies were on the verge of paying up, that his investment of £220 would lead to a yield of £12,000. Lizzie knew full well that such an eventuality was unlikely whereas Tom could not comprehend being "cheated."

Before the insurance companies could act, Lizzie did. Earlier, the proceeds of the insurance policy given by the Imperial had been assigned to a lawyer named Atkinson, to whom Tom owed a small sum of money, two or three hundred pounds. Atkinson agreed to forgive this debt, advance the sum of £810, and provide the services of another lawyer, one Acheson. The Wainewrights had to give additional surety in the form of the ownership of Linden House. In return for this, Acheson launched an action — a test case — against the Palladium on behalf of the destitute Madeleine Abercromby. Tom's interest in this particular policy was purely nominal: he acted as the indignant, self-righteous executor of Helen's estate.

The sum of £810 was crucial. Tom owed the crockery merchant Sharpus £610, due on 21 December. Cornwall, Sharpus' attorney, presented himself at Conduit Street, about an hour after my sister died. He pressed for payment, whereupon Tom allowed him to feast his eyes on the corpse and the various policies which had now fallen due as a result of her passing. Cornwall promised to inform his client of these changes in circumstances but suggested that Tom call upon the merchant in Cockspur Street. Tom did so that evening.

An exceedingly sharp-eyed entrepreneur who lived up to his name, Sharpus was not impressed. He noticed that Helen had made two wills: one leaving everything to Tom and the other bestowing everything to Madeleine. The merchant doubted that any of the Wainewright transactions would have an easy passage through Chancery. He insisted on payment within the week. Otherwise, he would go to the police. The other two hundred pounds were due to Wheatley, the auctioneer, for some recent purchases. The latter obligation could not be met.

When the insurance companies put their combined heads together, they sniffed rats and set their traps. Certain that Helen Abercromby had been poisoned, they acted in concert to repulse Thomas Wainewright, their common enemy. At first, Tom and Lizzie were pleased to have obtained the services of Acheson, but they soon became aware that none of the companies would pay up and that the Chancery proceedings would take years to resolve. They were now depleted of time and money, and the merchants of Turnham Green — who had not been paid off — sent bailiffs to Conduit Street. So did Sharpus.

Within five months, Tom's nerves — fraught at the best of times — snapped. He announced that he was going to "abandon" England until the Chancery suit was heard. He would go to France and await "developments." There was no question of Lizzie accompanying him. They now fought often and bitterly. Besides, she wanted to be close at hand to monitor developments, i.e., she wanted to be able to keep an eye on me. In May 1831 he sailed for Boulogne, and Lizzie, Griffiths, Sarah, and I moved to lodgings in Pimlico (Mrs. Gratton went into service in Chelsea).

In order to evade the bailiffs, our flight to Pimlico was under the cover of darkness. We did not move to the small terrace houses recently constructed there. Instead, our new set of rooms was in one of the "Neat Houses," the euphemistic expression for the sordid, dirty cottages erected in the early part of the seventeenth century. We were positioned a short distance from Watney's Stag Brewery and the public house known as *Jenny's Whim*. Once upon a time, the gardens at this pub were celebrated for their amusing deceptions, mechanical devices triggered by hidden springs. Out of the ground would pop harlequins, monsters, and other assorted predators to frighten unsuspecting female patrons. On the small lake floated models of mermaids and leaping fish. The extremely gullible and near-sighted were sometimes taken in by those devices. In my day, the only remnant of the lady's exotic fantasies resided in the now ramshackle establishment's name.

The four of us squeezed into three squalid rooms. Griffiths slept in a sleeping room whose walls and ceiling had huge marks — probably grease stains, Sarah and I barely fit into a chamber which had space only for our bed, and Lizzie occupied the largest of the small sleeping rooms. Meals were supposedly provided by Mrs. Astor, our landlady, but she, a connoisseur of gin, was often drunk. The little boy often went to sleep hungry, although Sarah and I did our best to force the slattern to provide us with our meals. The four of us had little to do but stroll in the neighbourhood but, within a few days, Lizzie did not even bother to do that. She was not distracted, simply withdrawn.

I began to take long promenades by myself. I required air not contaminated by Lizzie. As soon as I let myself out the front door, I would notice the two men — remarkably alike in their bald heads, round bodies, and tweed suits — who stood across the street from our entrance. One or both of them were always there — Lizzie told me they were the Forrester brothers, who, among other sordid activities, were bounty hunters. She told me that the consortium of insurance companies had likely hired them to "protect" us. Protect us from whom?, I wondered.

At first, my walks gave me a bit of comfort. On the second or third one, however, I noticed in the distance a young woman dressed in a bright yellow poplin. She walked slowly and, as I got closer, her hair and gait reminded me of Maddy. I became tearful, collected myself, and walked on. Just as drew level with her, I was certain she *was* Maddy. A few moments later, when I managed to overtake her, I looked back — the woman's countenance looked exactly like my own! I stopped, allowing the creature to continue ahead. Shaken by this encounter, I did not take the air for three days. Finally, I needed to escape for an hour. The three or four times I ventured forth, I again saw young women who bore unseemly likenesses to Madeleine; whenever I came directly upon them, they looked exactly like myself. Far too rational to believe in ghosts, visitations or hauntings, I put all this down to the hysterical spirits which had become my constant companions. Finally, I stopped wandering out on my own.

We did not have the comfort of any visitors until Henry Wheatley, the auctioneer, presented himself one afternoon. I answered the door. He was a tall, well-made young fellow, although his hair had touches of grey in it. I had once met him at Linden House. This time, he seemed embarrassed at encountering me. He muttered something about his sorrow

143

at my sister's death. Then, he paused and looked me straight in the eye. "I remember you as looking somewhat different" is all he could muster. I let him in and Lizzie, who was obviously expecting him, invited him into the sitting room. She asked if I would tend to Griffiths, but I explained that he had left an hour before with Sarah. I sat down, looked at the two of them, and waited for the conversation to unfold.

Wheatley had been summoned to Pimlico to inspect a number of small items which Lizzie had removed from Linden House, mainly intaglios and some small pieces of Bow porcelain. Lizzie, expecting to be able to rid herself of her debt to him, hoped he would sell the remainder of the items she presented for his purview. The auctioneer silently fondled each piece in turn and then glanced at Lizzie: "I regret to inform you, Madam, that these are counterfeits. All of them are forgeries." Before Lizzie could interject, he picked up the tiny cameo head of Flora.

Lizzie burst out: "Tom bought that from Richard Payne Knight, the antiquary."

"I daresay he did," Mr. Wheatley assured her. Then, his voice now taking on an air of confidence, he added: "But this piece has long been known to be the work of Benedetto Pistucci, the forger. I would have assumed a connoisseur of your husband's stature would not be so easily duped."

Mr. Wheatley gave me a careworn glance and announced his departure. He apologized for being the bearer of bad news and was about to leave the room, when he turned in my direction as if he were about to say something. He thought better of it, slowly rose to his feet, and left.

A week later, the post contained a letter to me from Mr. Wheatley. Could he meet with me at my earliest convenience? He suggested two days hence. Mystified, I wrote back to say I would receive him at the time he suggested. Lizzie was very apprehensive. What purpose could the auctioneer have in wishing to interview me?

When Mr. Wheatley arrived, he asked if I would walk out with him. Before he arrived, Lizzie, anxious to be a witness to any discussion I had with her husband's former associate, had foreseen this eventuality and ordered me to stay indoors. She would remain with us in the sitting room or, if Mr. Wheatley objected to this, she could easily eavesdrop from the comfort of her bedroom. As soon as Mr. Wheatley made his proposal, I assented. Lizzie found it difficult to hide her displeasure, but I pointed out to Mr. Wheatley that that very morning Lizzie had observed how pale I looked and how desperately I was in need of a promenade. My mendacity took her by surprise. She could only scowl.

Our walk that afternoon took us through Pimlico's desolate tracts of land and streets filled with warehouses and factories. Mr. Wheatley told me a curious story. He had a vivid memory of having encountered Madeleine and myself at Linden House. He had noticed that the two sisters bore a strong resemblance to each other, but he had been deeply attracted to the elder of the two, Helen. In fact, he had broken a self-imposed rule of never mixing business with pleasure; he had mentioned the matter to Mr. Wainewright. In turn, Tom had pointed out that Madeleine was by far the more beautiful of the two and that Helen's only claim to fame was a sharp, overly diligent intellect. In what I assume was his habitually self-effacing manner, Mr. Wheatley had disagreed with Tom. In fact, he told him that he was considering the possibility of "offering" to Helen. Tom then informed him that Helen was "reserved," that she was inseparable from her sister and would not entertain the possibility of marrying until her younger sister was settled.

A very discouraged Wheatley felt compelled to defer to Tom, the guardian of the two orphan girls. Soon after, he had been aggrieved to learn of Helen's death and was just recovering from this disappointment when he had encountered me the week before. He blushed and gulped for air before he could speak further.

At our last meeting, he had detected in my countenance much of the beauty he had once beheld in Helen's face. That response had confounded him: what kind of man simply transferred his allegiance from one sister to another? Why had he not previously been aware of my comeliness, which seemed to him now to surpass Helen's? Was — he wondered — callously substituting one woman for another?

Mr. Wheatley gulped once more. Honesty is, of course, a good thing, but I was overwhelmed that afternoon by the abundance that confronted me. When Mr. Wheatley beheld the tears gathering on my cheeks, he stopped speaking. Inadvertently, he then claimed, he had wounded me. He apologized. At the risk of hurting me further, he went on to say that he had vented his feelings because he wanted there to be no "deceit" between us. He wanted to "clear the ground" so that he could ask me to entertain the possibility of becoming his wife.

Reader, you cannot be more surprised than I was. As it was, I felt overwhelmed with divided feelings. First, my attention had indeed diverted itself onto Mr. Wheatley when I first beheld him at Linden House. I found his physiognomy compelling. I immediately brushed the matter aside because I was certain my feelings were not reciprocated and because, before her death, all my energy had been consumed in looking after Maddy. Second, I was still heavily inflicted with the sorrow and mystery of my sister's untimely death. Third, the remaining portion of my time was spent in determining how I was going to revenge myself on Lizzie, the only target close at hand. Fourth, why should I be touched by Mr. Wheatley's declaration? I had never been offered any evidence to suggest that men were anything but ruthless, feckless, or both. I felt that Mr. Wheatley was informing me that I was an attractive chattel, the genuineness of which had been momentarily in doubt.

My reaction to Mr. Wheatley might seem a bit calculated and thus cold, although I was touched at the revelation he had valued in my own right before the murder. As soon as I returned home, Lizzie demanded a summary of the conversation. Perfunctorily and sullenly, I told her that Wheatley had proposed and (I added a lie) that I had promised to give him a response within a few days.

Lizzie was beside herself with rage: how dare he make such a suggestion, one which would obviously inconvenience her? Before she could mount an attack on me, I informed her that I intended to marry Wheatley and that she would in no way interfere. If she tried to stop me, I would be forced to expose her. Moreover, if I were to die suddenly, any great expectations she had from the Courts of Chancery would be firmly dashed. That evening, I entered into an accord with her: I would retain my identity as Madeleine (a secret which would be kept from my husband), become a litigant in Chancery, and thus allow the lawsuit to reach a natural conclusion. In exchange, she would do nothing to block my departure from Pimlico.

I suppose a regard for one's comfort and safety is not a satisfactory rationale for contracting a marriage, but Mr. Wheatley's proposal allowed me to abandon Lizzie and, I sadly realized, that might be the best retribution I could exact. In one fell swoop, I obtained a modicum of economic stability and escaped her sharp claws.

I married Mr. Wheatley at St. James', Piccadilly, on 19 May 1832. I took Sarah with me to my new home in Knightsbridge. I felt sad at leaving my nephew behind (I never saw him again) but not even the slightest twinge of sorrow at bidding my half-sister adieu. I kept my word: my husband never knew my real name.

Three years after my marriage, on 29 June 1835, my petition against the Palladium was heard in Chancery. I attended only on the opening day and, upon taking my leave that afternoon, I am certain that I saw Lizzie, clad in black, disappearing down one of the corridors. Of course, the Palladium won and, under prodding from Lizzie, I initiated another (unsuccessful) action against the Eagle in December 1836. The remainder of my life as a living fake is not worthy of your scrutiny. My husband died in a post-chaise accident on 12 September 1837. Left with three young children, I became mortally ill with scarlet fever two years later.

My biography is of interest only because I was a witness to a dreadful series of murders. I shall spare you an account of how crushingly sad I was rendered when I became fully aware that I was going to die, leaving behind two girls and a boy, all under the age of five. I never endured greater anguish than that which came from the certainty that I would soon take my leave of those three cherubs. During those agonizing moments, my mind frequently drifted back to Maddy and myself as young children. I recalled the simple happiness which Maddy took in my company, how she sometimes mistakenly called me "momma." I died in my twenty-ninth year on 25 September 1839.

part six
Eliza

Helen has complained at nauseous length about her invisibility. Her existence after 1830 — although I admit it is under an assumed name — is extremely well documented. The same cannot be said for me. In the course of the first Chancery proceedings, the Attorney-General accused me of murder but the presiding magistrate, the gentlemanly Lord Talfourd, countered by suggesting that he was indulging in "pleasurable associations." When that action failed, I beseeched Helen to bring a second action against one of the insurance companies. This, she did.

Shortly after Helen's departure from Pimlico, Griffiths and I moved to 24 Palace New Road, Lambeth. As far as the archival records are concerned, my subsequent life is entirely a matter of conjecture. After alluding to the fact that I was successful in persuading a journalist into not writing about me (so pitiful was my existence), one historian then voices these speculations:

> Mrs. Wainewright is said to have emigrated to Boston in America with her son in 1851, and to have died there. Young Griffiths threw up a promising career in the Navy to accompany her. He is rumoured to have inherited his father's talent for painting, and to have returned to England in order to study art, after marrying a woman of means. But there are no facts to support these assertions — and little hope, at this date, of discovering the truth.

You will note the skilful construction of the above paragraph: I am given a perfunctory sentence and then the spotlight is thrown on my son. In the public record, men are central, women — if they are lucky — mere afterthoughts. Some things never change.

Did the leopard manage, you are wondering, to remove her spots? I have never been able to comprehend why Madeleine ordered Helen not to touch the oysters and then swallowed them herself. Had she heard the rumour (a true one) of Tom's parallel pursuit — unauthorized by me — of a Norfolk heiress, whom he serenaded with a Spanish guitar one night in Mecklenburgh Square? Did she have second thoughts about allowing the imperious Helen to perish? Did she — for some unknown reason — want to die?

Whatever her motivation, Madeleine's decision placed me in yet another sticky situation. As you may have discerned, I introduced strychnine — for me, the classical poison — into the oysters. After Maddy's foolhardy behaviour — foreseeing the outlandish complications which would confront me — I laboured to save her life. I did not meddle with the black dose or the subsequent (expensive) medicines ordered in by Locock. My suspicion is that those drugs interacted with the remnants of strychnine in her system and thus led to my half-sister's

know, the niceties involved in copying the work of others. From the time of my arrival in London, I attended many sales at the auction houses and at the few exhibitions of paintings, engravings, and sculpture open to the public. So by 1830, I had a skilful hand and a well-trained eye. I became a forger.

My first independent effort in the "manufacturing" way was an unsigned — but unmistakeable — Titian, a lovely landscape burnished with purple hills and gold-filled sky. The radiant colours of the world as only the inner eye of an artist can render it. Two shepherds, engaged in a rambling conversation, seem oblivious of their surroundings, their forgetfulness making the viewer poignantly aware of how ordinary the unnaturally beautiful can be for those who are content to live within the comforts of nature.

Making the picture was comparatively easy — selling it another matter. I hired a dray to convey the canvas, carefully wrapped in the finest sheepskin, to Christie's on King Street. The accompanying missive was from one Miss Smith, a distressed gentlewoman, explaining that this glorious item had been in her family for nearly a hundred years. Due to the extenuating circumstance of poverty, she had overcome her reluctance to part with it. Would the auction house act on her behalf?

Two days later, I made my way to the imposing portals of that firm. My Miss Smith was clad in black silk. Not the finest quality of silk but one appropriate for a proud woman whose circumstances had been severely reduced. The only remnant of past glory was a tiny ivory brooch, the representation of Flora spurned by Wheatley. My hair, *en chignon*, was a deep auburn-red. I allowed a small bit of curl to escape the confines I had imposed, a hint of the turmoil that filled me with the prospect of surrendering a family keepsake.

As soon as I made my way through the small entranceway, I entered a hall stuffed to bursting with all manner of curiosities: a baby giraffe which some cruel hunter had deprived of life and which a kind-hearted taxidermist had managed to make look both poignant and awkward; huge wooden barrels filled with damp straw — these were presumably the temporary homes of various pieces of china; the walls on both sides were filled with every manner of oil and etching; about ten Greek gods and goddesses stood idly by, some with missing arms and various other organs. Only one was missing a head.

The porter who waited on me did not seem to know anything of the painting submitted by Miss Smith. "I shall have to check with the proper authority, Madam." He drifted away, leaving me to my own devices in that whirling dervish of a room. Fifteen minutes later he returned, accompanied by a scruffy-looking, odoriferous young man. "Theo, accompany the lady to the chambers of Mr. Albright." We walked down all manner of corridors until we reached a part of the vast building which seemed uninhabited. None of the innumerable doors were marked, but this did not bother my companion. Suddenly, he stopped, knocked, and took his leave when the occupant of that chamber opened the door.

Mr. Albright ushered me into his room, the chasteness of which stood in stark contrast to the hullabaloo I had earlier witnessed. The few furnishings were all Hepplewhites: a small settee, two sitting chairs. The curtains were drawn, and the only illumination in the room surrounded the easel occupied by my Titian. Mr. Albright was a man of medium height, his colouring and hair indicating he was a man of sixty years. He had a worried smile, but that did not enter into his speech.

"Miss Smith, sit down. Can I offer you any refreshment? Sherry? Port?" I declined. My refusal did not impede him. He poured himself a huge helping of port and then sat down opposite me, so that we both could behold the Titian, quite happily at home in its new sanctuary.

"Miss Smith, your Titian is of the most exquisite nature. Its beauty overwhelms me. I cannot keep my eyes from it, but in many other ways it disturbs — nay frightens — me. At first, I was convinced it was a forgery. You see the

153

hillocks there and that stand of trees. Can only be Umbria. Titian never painted there."

Small, meaningful pause. "So I was convinced that I would have to give you bad news this afternoon. Now, I am not so sure." He took a deep breath as if about to speak but only a small supply of "uhhmms" and "hmms" escaped his lips. He exhaled again.

"This picture flies against all my knowledge of the dear Venetian's life, simply destroys countless assumptions I have made over many years of study. The life of a connoisseur can be arduous — he gives so much of himself to the work of others. Every logical deduction this expert can make" — he pointed in the direction of his heart — "tells me this picture cannot be a Titian." Another significant pause. His eye filled with tears. "But then I become overwhelmed — drowned — by the greatness of what has been accomplished here. Only a genius of Titian's calibre could have achieved this. I surrender to its greatness. We will offer it for sale. It will fetch a goodly sum."

The remainder of my conversation with Mr. Albright was confined to a discussion of the picture's provenance, of how one of my grandfathers had tutored Lord F, the legendary collector, at Cambridge, subsequently becoming his Librarian. The picture had been a small gift when Lord F was dying and had therefore not entered any of the lists of his innumerable collections. Mr. Albright seemed satisfied. I rose to take my leave. He stood as if about to take my hand, but, before he did so, he swung his head round in the direction of the picture once again. He gave a loud sigh. "These geniuses break all the rules we lesser mortals try to impose on them. Fortunately, I know Titian well enough to recognize his hand in even this unusual setting. Maybe the chap went there on holiday, didn't think enough of the place to make a whole raft of pictures." Then, he turned to face me. "We are so grateful to you for thinking of us." My Titian and the candles gave the room even more of a strange, otherworldly glow as Mr. Albright curtsied me out in farewell and benediction.

As I strolled back through the hall crammed to bursting, I looked again at all those treasures leaving one collection to go on to yet another. I felt a tinge of sadness for the sad life of those objects, never finding refuge in a permanent home. All those things, forever wandering, always destined to go somewhere else, unless by lucky chance they got broken or destroyed by fire or water. I wondered if the various busts, funerary tombs, elaborate brocades, pieces of armour at the British Museum ever felt at home, or did they feel unvalued, clustered uneasily together?

Mine has always been a spirit that takes pleasure in the ephemeral. That day, I was chastened, reflecting on how an elementary mistake had almost given me away. Attend to detail, attend to detail, I reminded myself. Although I possessed an iron constitution, narrow escapes always gave me palpitations.

Forging is not very different from poisoning. Both are the acts of artists, although not in the commonplace way in which that profession is traditionally comprehended. All painters impose order through their art and — in the process — suggest that their arrangement is more interesting and more pleasing than nature. Thus, painters are — by their natures — extremely arrogant. They are confidence artists. Of course, I realize, there are those painters who, like my husband, are excellent forgers but miserable artists.

The poisoner removes an obstacle in nature in order to introduce symmetry into her life. She does this on the quiet, for hers is a profession whose artistry must remain undetected. The same holds true for the forger: if she is truly adept at her profession, her artistry is never discovered, remains invisible, and is thus erased.

There are crucial distinctions between the two callings. Forgery is certainly more respectable. Without doubt, it is a cut above being a whore or an actress. Nevertheless, these two callings — which are often confused with each other — bear a superficial resemblance to my own two vocations in that in all four *form* is privileged over *content*. Can the actress imitate a certain emotion? Can the whore convince the john that she is taking pleasure in their act? Can the poisoner induce the police into concluding that a normal death occurred? Can the forger charm a buyer into believing that an object is authentic?

For me, the great irony of my vocation was that I had to replicate, for the most part, the work of men. There were no female artists to copy. So, as a woman, I had an arduous task ahead of me. I had to leave my femininity behind in order to copy the works of men and — and this is crucial — I had to be a better artist than, say, Rembrandt or Raphael.*

Rosa Corder is the best-known woman forger. By definition, her renown makes her a consummate failure in her profession. She was born on 18 May 1853, the sixth child of Micah Corder, a lighterman. Rosa's family was musical — one of her brothers helped to popularize Wagner in England. Rosa, who was educated at Boulogne, later received instruction in art from Felix Moschler. In 1879, she displayed a portrait of her mother at the Royal Academy, but her speciality was animal paintings of horses and dogs. A would-be Stubbs.

To make ends meet, Rosa posed for Whistler. One of his most successful arrangements in black and brown is of her. In a book from 1919, the lady's dubious status in the art world is

---

*EDITOR'S NOTE: Forgive my presumptuousness, but I think Eliza is telling us that forgery is a profession to which many are called but few are chosen. Leaving that issue aside, she is also reminding us in a general way that one can never be too careful. In recent years, as I read in *Newsweek*, one monumental sculptural forgery was a copy based on a Greek bronze statuette of a warrior of 470 BC, only five inches high and located in the Antikenabteilung, Berlin. The forgers made an eight-foot-high reproduction of it in terra cotta and offered it as an Etruscan masterpiece. The resemblance was noted by the experts, who thought it to be an example of an Etruscan artist borrowing a Greek design motif. (Very clever to mix two time frames thus.) In 1961, after it had been in the Metropolitan Museum of Art in New York for forty years, an analysis was made of the black glaze that covered the figure. It was found that the glaze contained as a colouring agent manganese, which never was used for this purpose in ancient times. Finally, Alfredo Adolfo Fioravanti confessed that he was the sole survivor of three forgers who had contrived this "unique" masterpiece.

hastily sketched. "Rosa Corder, a gifted and beautiful woman, was Whistler's favourite model and lived for a time on very intimate terms with him. She is also declared to have been on terms with Rossetti and later on with Charles Howell. His influence on her was terrible and far-reaching." Rosa wanted to be a painter and wound up becoming a sex-slave. The "terms" of a single woman's existence are very restricted — in language and in practice. Not much news there. She was influenced — women are always written about in passive voice. *Absolutely* no news there.

So Rosa was a hand-me-down from Whistler to Rossetti to Charles Howell. The latter you will not find in the *Dictionary of National Biography* or *Chambers*. He was a man of very mysterious origins, supposedly born in Oporto in 1840 to William Howell, an English artist and his wife, Dona Enriqueta Amelia de Souza de Rosa Coelho, a member of the Portuguese nobility. At the age of seventeen, the handsome and sexually ambidextrous young man arrived in London, became "innocently" involved in a scandal, and left England after a year's stay. Supposedly — although there is little evidence for this — he manipulated a serving woman to poison her employer.

He was gone for seven years. What happened during those years? According to one source, he passed the time in the most romantic of ways, supporting his mother and sisters by diving for treasures off of a sunken galleon he had impulsively purchased. This proving not altogether a lucrative pursuit, he emigrated to Morocco, became the sheik of an Arab tribe, passed day and night in the saddle, and after having rendered various services to the Portuguese government — for whom he acted as a spy — returned to England and became secretary to John Ruskin, whom he supposedly seduced. Realistically, all this sounds a bit far-fetched, but it is an exciting story. What seems more certain is that Howell, who, at various times, worked as an interior decorator, railway engineer, secretary, and agent, exerted his handsome physiognomy and physique on all those whom he met. He became Rossetti's confidant. Perhaps Howell is best remembered as the person who convinced Rossetti to exhume the body of Lizzy Siddal in order to retrieve the poetical manuscripts which he had precipitously flung into his wife's grave. For that service, students of literature must be forever grateful to that wonderful scoundrel.

Of course, Charles was a gifted entrepreneur, who subsequently persuaded Miss Corder to undertake a number of canvases in the Rossetti-style, that artist having abandoned painting at a comparatively early age. Students of art hate Howell because he has undeniably caused major ructions in the establishment of the provenance of Rossetti's paintings and drawings. This prince of scoundrels received his comeuppance by the unsavoury manner of his death in 1890. T.J. Wise, himself one of the great forger-bunglers, left this account:

> He was found early one morning lying in the gutter outside a public-house in Chelsea. His throat was badly cut, and a ten-shilling piece was tightly wedged between his clenched teeth. He was removed to the Home Hospital, Fitzroy Square. Here he lingered a few days, sufficient to render it possible for the cause of death to be mercifully certified as pneumonia phthisis, from which disease he was suffering at the time.

So even the cause of Howell's death was forged, his entire life a cheat. Howell was a rogue upon whom the servants of literature and art finally took their revenge.

Rosa's life — and reputation — was ruined because she fell in love with an amoral brute. She allowed her feelings to get in her way — and corrupt her. She became the inamorata of a forger who used — and then discarded — her. Howell could not draw or paint, but he was addicted to those who could. And he knew that a great deal of money could be exacted by the right salesperson, with access to a commodity which was no longer in production. During the years she was infatuated with Howell, Rosa produced excellent likenesses of paintings which Rossetti had made when he was infatuated with Lizzy, whose death brought those productions to a halt.

Many of Rosa's forgeries have escaped detection and are now attributed to Rossetti. A wonderful irony is at work: Rosa's imitations were, in large part, generated by her passion for Charles Howell whereas the institutions which own her Rossettis claim that they own portraits of Lizzy which manifest Rossetti's passion for the sitter. Now, I suppose, Rosa could have been part-lesbian and fallen in love with Lizzy. The question is: where does the passion reside in a work of art if a forger can so readily simulate it? Like Tom Wainewright, Rosa was an indefatigable forger of Fuseli erotica. Maybe there was some real emotion in those works? Perhaps she and Charles practised what they preached?

In the 1830s, the Charles Howell–Rosa Corder liaison had not yet taken place. I did not have the benefit of hindsight, but I was perfectly well aware that any forger must remain aloof from emotional attachment and start small. So I placed tiny Titian, Poussin, and Lorraine pieces in at Christie's. As you already know, I identified myself under a variety of false names to the so-called "experts" and, *de rigueur*, those pieces were offered as "The Property of a Lady" or "The Property of a Gentlewoman." I noticed that the various officials with whom I dealt had no real interest in my identity — only in that of the work of art under discussion.

After my encounter with Mr. Albright, I lived in Putney and was the impoverished daughter of a Brigadier-General; at other times, I was the offspring of a long-deceased scholar who, while faithfully and diligently discharging his office as a Keeper at the British Museum, had been able to acquire minor works by important artists for a fraction of their real worth. Of course, my hair-colouring and face powders also underwent the appropriate metamorphoses.

Forgery is a profession which requires a lot of attention to detail and, as such, is essentially feminine. In time, I came to resent the imposition of male values on my calling. I found a way around this ticklish situation by mothering a number of important works under the name of Artemisia Gentileschi, born in Rome in 1593 to the painter Orazio Gentileschi, who trained his daughter to follow his profession. A scoundrel named Agostino Tassi promised to marry the young woman and, under this pretext, received sexual favours from her. She enjoyed her lover, but, when he refused to marry her, she and her father brought an action against him. She was subsequently tortured, and Tassi's trial for rape was inconclusive. The abortive trial left Artemisia nothing but her talent. She had no choice but to take advantage of that fact.

I first came upon the work of this extraordinary woman when I beheld that portion of the decorations of the Queen's House at Greenwich which she helped her father decorate in 1637, when she made her only trip to England. In Artemisia I beheld a woman after my own heart, and I knew that her name would give me the licence to paint the kind of picture I now had to undertake. I wanted to devise pictures about strong, self-reliant Amazons who do not need men; in fact, I wanted to create canvases in which feminine power rejects the masculine imperative.

That is how I came to do my Judith pictures (*Judith Beheading Holofernes*, oil on canvas, 169 x 162 cm, Galleria degli Uffizi, and *Judith and her Maidservant*, oil on canvas 185.2 x 141.6 cm, The Detroit Institute of Arts). Before, in Renaissance art, Judith's self-empowering gesture had been handled in an overly decorative, almost cozy manner. In the earlier representations, Judith wears a party frock which has no blood stains, or she looks at the decapitated bully as if her actions and his death had nothing to do with each other. My Judith canvases are about women, power, and violence. Sometimes, they suggest, women must take vengeance upon those persons who mistreat them. There are situations in which the only satisfactory riposte for a woman is a physically violent one. If you fail to make such a response, you remain a nonentity.

I undertook a third canvas by this remarkable painter: *Self-Portrait as "The Art of Painting,"* oil on canvas, 96.5 x 73.7 cm, now owned by Her Majesty the Queen. Here you can see my strong, steady gaze keenly studying a subject and my brush dexterously attacking the subject in front of me.

My Artemisia pictures are my proudest productions: each is in a major collection in a different country. As well, they are true acts of sisterhood in which my identity as an artist blends into the Italian woman's.*

I did not emigrate to America, as some of the Wainewright biographers insist. I simply re-invented myself as a Lady. I must add that I am *somewhat* proud of my son Griffiths, who did enter the Navy but never lived in Boston. He is known to all of you under the name of George Gordon DeLuna Byron who, justifiably ashamed of his own father, claimed to be the natural son of Lord Byron and his consort, the Countess DeLuna, whose secret marriage contravened the laws of England and Spain. The Major — as he was briefly known — was a peerless forger of Romantic documents, particularly of letters by Byron, Shelley, and Keats. The good tidings: my son's Keats letters are much more beautifully phrased than the poet's own surviving letters. Without doubt, they are much more genuinely Keatsian. The bad news: William White, one of the many booksellers to whom Griffiths sold, discovered the ruse and presented the incriminating documents to the British Museum (now Library), where the evidence of my poor son's subterfuges is immortalized in the Manuscripts Room. Griffiths was too much his father's child. I completed my life in considerable ease. I died of old age in London on 12 May 1875.

---

*EDITOR'S NOTE: Eliza Wainewright can take some of the credit for the glory celebrated in Germaine Greer's prose: "For the woman of today, Artemisia represents the female equivalent of an Old Master. She is the exception to all the rules: she rejected a conventional feminine rôle for a revolutionary female one."

Once again, my parents have made spectacles of themselves. More than slightly exhibitionistic in their lifetimes, they are compelled to repeat that past. I cannot dissociate myself completely from them.

Attached to every life is a catalogue of feigned emotions. Most of us practise some form of faking. We all pretend politeness when we encounter someone we dislike but whom we do not wish to know of our disdain. Many people "adjust" their tax returns. Most women have at some point faked an orgasm, a talent which males cannot realistically hope to emulate.

Poisoning people and forging paintings are in an entirely different league from the usual detritus of life. I grant that, but I have to tread cautiously in this area. I made my way in the world under an assumed name. My mother has observed that I was, in my choice of a profession, my parents' genuine offspring. True enough. But I did rebel in a small way: I never forged paintings — only letters and poems.

Childhood, as we now know it, was largely manufactured by treacly Victorian sentimentality. In the early nineteenth century, children were simply little men and women, not small creatures with sensibilities — and thus sensitivities — of a vastly different order from grown-ups. Even by those standards, I had an exceedingly unhappy boyhood.

I wish I could speak with any kind of authority about the Wainewright murders. I remember almost nothing, having not yet reached my third year when my aunt died. I have imprecise remembrances of the grown-ups: floods of tears, flayings of hands, whispered but nevertheless terror-stricken snippets of conversation. My surviving aunt — not as friendly as the other one — would read to me in my room, but the stories would cease abruptly when her eyes suddenly became too moist for her to see anything on the page.

What I do recall was the terrifying sense of unease which now invaded me on a regular basis. I was not used to a stable environment, but anxiety now became a constant companion. As I wandered the flat, no one had time for me. My mother, strikingly beautiful in the way her body was topped by masses of auburn hair, did not dress until early evening. She simply spent most of daylight in bed, the sheets drawn up over her head. When she finally arose, she wore a cotton chemise which trailed on to the ground. My aunt was perfectly attired — in the dark blues and greys she favoured — from early in the day. Tom's clothing was in a constant state of agitation: his trousers rumpled, his shirts soiled. Then, he vanished. I retain virtually no memory of him.

Of the actual move to Pimlico I have no recollection. What I can still vaguely recall are the rooms there. Extremely small, but in a peculiar way: they were abbreviated in length, none more than eight feet, but the really odd thing was their width: five feet at the most. That is my persistent recollection. And, of course, the subdued tension was constant, occasionally rising to an angry exchange between my mother and her half-sister. For the most part, they were content to snipe at each other and then relapse into silence. Then, Madeleine also vanished. I never saw her again. My mother became slightly more subdued, although she was a fidgety, restless woman, forever commencing one activity, forgetting it, taking up another and then returning to the abandoned project.

One day, she informed me I was to accompany her into the City. "I shall be Mrs. Endicott today, you will be my son, Nigel. You are not to intrude into any conversation. Is that understood, little sir?" I nodded my head in agreement.

My mother wore the mourning dress purchased two years before for her half-sister's funeral. A small bonnet of the same colour decked her head, whence a thin veil fell down to cover her face. The outfit signified that the wearer was a recent widow whose circumstances had been severely reduced. There was another touch: the dress was of no consequence, but the hat — recently shoplifted from a milliner on Bond Street — was of supreme quality. "I am a person of considerable, even expensive taste," the costume design proclaimed, "but I cannot any longer completely live up to my own standards." A powerful message when one is selling something in the art world.

Our destination was Colnaghi's, the print dealers, in Berkeley Square. There, the liveried doorman helped us out of the shabby carriage we had hired for our journey. My mother told the driver to return in an hour. Once in the door, my mother ordered one of the attendants to summon Mr. Ralph. Almost immediately, a young man approached, salaamed profusely, and paid his compliments. He was nineteen at most and had a decidedly awkward air about him. Modestly outfitted in dark green cloth, the silk of his cravat had worn through at the edges. He invited us to accompany him to a small corner of the enormous foyer. There, a small table —

probably a Chippendale because I can still remember the subdued but very red tones of the mahogany — awaited us.

"Madam, as I told you in my missive, Colnaghi & Co. are delighted to have the privilege of examining your Dürer etching." He proclaimed this in a tone which indicated that he was no longer Mr. Ralph; rather, he had transformed himself into an assemblage of persons, the safety of the firm.

My mother was supposed to be impressed and so she assumed the appropriate — grovelling — emotions. "As I informed you, I am uncertain of this etching. My husband acquired it at a provincial auction many years ago, well before we were married. It looks authentic, but I know there are many forgeries about."

"Yes, madam. That is unfortunately true. As Colnaghi knows from bitter experience."

Without further fuss, my mother handed him the small, thin parcel she was holding. Mr. Ralph salaamed again and then proceeded slowly to remove the layers of tissue in which the etching was embedded. Finally, he held it by one of its corners. Then, he waved it, as if it was a small carpet from which he hoped to expel dust. Then, he placed it flat down on the table and proceeded to rub his wrist against the surface, almost like a lover trying to stimulate the flesh of his beloved. Satisfied, he turned the etching over and proceeded to place the tips of his fingers upon the surface of the etching. Then, from somewhere on his person, he extracted a magnifying glass, with which he scanned the image. Finally, he put away that instrument and rather hurriedly took a glance at the etching.

"A magnificent piece of work. Absolutely of the first magnitude."

My mother smiled.

Mr. Ralph returned the compliment. With a gleam in his eye, he looked at her. "This is a pristine rendition of the first state of *Melancholia*. Colnaghi has never beheld anything like this before. The paper is right, the etching cuts deeply into the paper as it should, the ink glows."

My mother nodded for him to go on. She could feel —
almost taste — the many guineas just about to be placed in
her hand.

Colnaghi coughed, although it looked as if Mr. Ralph
had done so. This was to signify a change in the direction of
the conversation. "The problem is that the etching is *too*
perfect. Dürer engravings never exist in such a state. The
image has never been placed in a frame. Perhaps it has
always been hidden away in the drawers of the various
collectors who have owned it? That's a guess, but, on the
whole, we are certain this example is a fake."

The "we" was extremely oppressive. This was not simply
one expert's judgement. The whole weight of Colnaghi had
turned itself against us.

Mother tried to appear nonplussed. "How can you say
an etching is a forgery because it is too perfect?"

Mr. Ralph beamed, his countenance alive with
benignity. "Madam, we at Colnaghi long ago learned that
the condition of sublunary man is one of gross
imperfection." He had now become a lecturer in aesthetics,
a professor of moral philosophy. He was not to be dissuaded.
"We always worry terribly if we are shown any piece of art
which seems to be in absolutely pristine condition. Our
experience is that such objects are by copyists possessing a
perverted genius."

My mother, a supreme realist, knew when she was
beaten. Mr. Ralph accompanied us to the door, bestowing
upon us his final salaam. We waited a few minutes for our
carriage to draw up and then began the drive back to
Pimlico. My sullen mother crumpled the small parcel, tore
it into about a dozen pieces and dispatched it out the
window to join the layers of debris that littered the London
street. I think I caught the word "bungler" escape her lips.

I lived with my mother until I could obtain work at the age
of twelve. Perhaps not surprisingly, my first job was as a
porter at Christie's. That is, I was a jack of all trades in
lifting, moving, and lugging about various kinds of objects

within the rabbit warrens where all the various commodities were stored. After I had been there two years, I was given the privilege of attending in the comparative elegance of the auction rooms. There, I would lift pieces of porcelain well above my head, almost as if I were a priest at the Offertory of the Roman Catholic mass. Or, I would be one of two, three, or four lads who trooped into the rooms to display canvases.

Early on, I developed a deep repulsion for the visual arts. Reading was my pleasure, especially the intricate, baroque weavings of Sir Thomas Browne and his fellow seventeenth-century wordsmiths. I had little affection for novels, always preferring the security of the factual. Another passion was the great poetry of my own time: Keats, Shelley, Byron. Little Mr. Symington — the only "expert" who displayed a semblance of kindness to the porters — was not held in high esteem by his colleagues. He specialized in books and manuscripts, which did not at that time sell for large sums.

A short, squat man with bristles sprouting profusely out of his bald head, nose, and ears, he had little regard for the other "authorities." Like me, he was more interested in the intricacies of cursive writing, in the various ways in which ink touched, splattered, and sometimes blotched a supposed letter by Shakespeare or a court document signed by Queen Elizabeth. He taught me about inks, how they were manufactured, about their countless variations; he also loved paper, especially their watermarks, their supposed guarantee of authenticity.

Mr. Symington exposed many notorious forgers, among them George Psalmanazar, the Frenchman, who immigrated to England where he pretended, with great success, to be a native of Formosa and published a book about that island, which he had never visited.

From Mr. Symington, I learned that the only lasting love in this world is that of the reader for the writer who is willing to bare his soul and, in consequence, display the wonders of this fragile human world. Or the love some have for the artists who show the splendours of the human face or a landscape. No love is more pure, shores us up against the vicissitudes of life.*

One day, Mr. Symington called me aside. "Lad, I have noticed your fascination with the seemingly dull pieces of paper which are my charge."

"Yes, sir," I replied deferentially. "They have their own special beauty."

"That shows remarkable refinement in one so young."

"Not so much refinement as inclination."

"A good thing. Have you a favourite as yet? Shakespeare, Spenser, Marvell?"

"Not really. I am still settling into them."

"It took me a long while to settle on a special person. Strangely enough, a modern. The mad poet, Cowper. He has been dead only forty years."

"I've never read any of the letters, only that long poem, *The Task*."

"Most people are in your predicament. I'll show you some letters to his friend, Unwin, which will be on offer within the fortnight." My mentor pushed a handful in my direction and waited patiently while I perused them. When he saw a smile cross my face, he injected: "Exactly. A very playful sense of humour thriving in the midst of acute melancholia. You'll notice how beautifully the words are formed, almost mirroring his elegant soul. Hardly ever does he scratch out a word or a sentence. The pieces of paper are art works in their own right."

I bowed in agreement.

---

*EDITOR'S NOTE: Some of these love affairs go to truly astonishing extremes, as happened at the huge van Gogh retrospective at the Museum of Modern Art a few years ago. One devotee went several times but could not look at the canvases properly, so crowded was the room. So, he purchased a sow's ear from a butcher, placed it in an elegant box, labelled it as the severed ear van Gogh had posted to Gauguin, and smuggled box and its contents into the Museum, where, stealthily, he placed it in the immediate vicinity of the paintings. Of course, all the visitors immediately vacated the canvases in favour of the ear, and the perpetrator of this harmless prank got to see the pictures unobstructedly. He loved the art but knew that the hoi polloi were interested in only the freak show side of the Dutch artist's tragic life.

"I knew you'd see that."

My career as a forger began more by accident than by design when I wondered if it would be possible to pass a letter of my own devising as one by Cowper. On Piccadilly, I wandered in and out of several stationers until I was able to find one which had a stock of fifty-year-old writing paper, bearing one of the watermarks the insane poet had employed. That was not easily done. Even more difficult was to find ink of the right texture and colour. Although ink had not changed much since Cowper's time, obtaining the right colour was a chore. This done, I sat down to write my missive, deciding it would be a letter to his cousin, Lady Hesketh, to whom Cowper had penned his most whimsical letters. I almost wrote "Harriet" rather than employing her own eccentric spelling of her name, "Harriot." Luckily, I caught myself in time. I let myself go, unleashing a cascade of comic staccato moments tinged with sadness. I scratched out only one word and signed the letter with what I thought was the appropriate gusto.

The next day, I approached Mr. Symington at the start of the day. In an agitated fashion, I spoke of having come across a letter from Cowper loosely enclosed in a copy of *The Task* I had come upon at one of the numerous stalls in the Strand. In his excitement, Mr. S snatched the sheet from my hand, in the process almost ripping it. He scoured it quickly and then went back over it slowly. He looked for the proper watermark, which he soon found. "Exactly. One of the greatest of all Cowper letters." My proceeds from the sale were the enormous sum of ten guineas. My career was in flight.

I was never a "creative" writer in the ordinary sense of that adjective. Starting from scratch, the blank paper remained such. However, I could begin the difficult process by attaching myself, much in the manner of a limpet, to the writings of others. I could never be "original" but I could be "imitative." So, if I immersed myself in the writings of, say, Wordsworth, I could within a week or so completely enter into his poetical identity, making his soul my own. Then, I was in business, able to rhyme off all kinds of wonderful pieces of verse and prose which have sometimes been judged better than the writings of the person imitated.

A strange talent this form of amusement. Stranger even to have to enter into the complete identities of others in order to do it. But if the love we bestow on writers is essentially unconditional, my affection transcended those bounds. I was so much in love with my beloveds, I allowed every ounce of their beings to penetrate me. Some people would say I was a person of little talent who cannibalized my betters. There is an element of truth in that. Nevertheless, I would like you to look at the other side of the coin: the complete self-abnegation and surrender of myself to the geniuses of my "authors."

For me, imitation remained the sincerest form of flattery. In my twenties, I began to style myself George Gordon DeLuna Byron and maintained that my mother, a Spanish lady by the name of the Countess DeLuna, had contracted a secret marriage to Byron. I added the sobriquet of "Major" to signify, untruthfully, I had served a stint with the East India Company. Now, I did leave a large, obvious clue in my wake. Luna = Lunacy. Those who wish to be deceived are hard to dissuade from that inclination.

Some would maintain that I outrageously perverted the course of English literary history by creating a series of documents which distort the life records of almost all the great medieval, renaissance, and age-of-reason writers. My bias runs in a completely different direction. I have spiced those dull histories with all kinds of improbable happenings, wonderful byways, sources of fascination. Chaucer found guilty of rape? Marlowe's murder? Pope's adventures in a whore house? You can lay such lively events at my door. In the process, you might consider gratitude rather than anger. You may even wish to utter a word of thanks to me for enlivening what otherwise would be drab lives. My pleasure may have been my business, but I also performed inestimable service to the literature of my nation.

171

Unless you are someone of considerable inanity, you must respect the trouble I went to in order to give the exact sense of truth to my productions. Imagine the tedious hours I spent at the British Museum glancing at the various folios and quartos of Shakespeare until a distracted attendant turned his attention away for a few seconds, whereupon I razored out a page in order to "salt" it into one of my finds (if one is ever questioned about a fake's identity, one brazenly suggests that page x suffer a battery of tests — when the genuine page passes with flying colours, no more doubts can be entertained as to the authenticity of the entire volume). Consider the stress of waiting in the Manuscript Room to steal one or two letters by Byron in order to have an authentic piece or two planted amongst a newly found batch of letters. The labour is great, the reward is scanty in comparison.

The work can also be exceedingly dangerous. There is a reasonable safety in announcing a "newly discovered" pamphlet or broadside by Coleridge or Wordsworth. Since there is nothing extant to which to compare such a "discovery," the experts are content to look at the physical evidences of authenticity. Then, they turn their attention to the contents. Does this read like the early Coleridge? Are the vocabulary, stylistic mannerisms, and tropes such as to suggest that the young poet could have written this? On such matters, opinions of necessity vary. Very dangerous is the discovery of a new batch of letters by Byron because — unless the forger has had access to every one of the thousands of missives he scribbled — it is easy to make a mistake. For example, Byron may have been known to be at Cheltenburgh on a day I place him in Edinburgh. Or, he could have been bedding Lady C_____ on the very evening I have him in the arms of a Soho whore.

My first set of troubles began early on when, at the age of seventeen, I was summoned to the Chiswick manor of the widow, Julia Puddicombe. Her well-furnished sitting room was dotted with mementoes of the poet: a few locks of hair in small frames, some copies of the well-known oils, all manner of Byron imprints on the tops of various cabinets. Pride of place was given to three pencil sketches of the poet signed by Thomas Phillips, the portraitist. An outrageously tall person clothed in deepest black, the lady started catechizing me as soon as I was seated.

"The rumour I have heard — contradict me if I am wrong — is that you claim to be the natural offspring of Byron."

"Not a flight of fancy, Madam. A fact."

"Indeed. Tell me how this is so."

I recited for her my lineage, embellishing it with facts and circumstances intended to build up the semblance of reasonableness. I had been born in 1824, in the last year of the poet's life. Her eyes flashing at each turn in my tale, she found it difficult to hold her tongue. I feared she would unmask me as an impostor by observing that I could not possibly have reached my twenty-first year.

Finally, she could contain herself no longer. "Strange there are no letters from the poet to the lady." I was delighted to have located the source of her agitation.

"But, Madam, there are. Ten or eleven, as I remember."

"Ten or eleven??"

"Indeed, I have them in the safekeeping of a friend in France."

Her tiny eyes widened, attempting to take all this in. She mused: "Ten or eleven." Then, those startled eyes became tranquil, as if she had entered a state of reverie. At that moment, I knew the widow's weeds were not for the late Mr. Puddicombe but for the scoundrel-poet. She drew her back up, collected herself, adjusted the sleeves on both arms, and was ready to speak again.

"I would very much like to see those letters, would you allow me the privilege?"

"Madam, I regret this is not really possible. I have offered them to a dealer. In fact, I leave for France in a fortnight to retrieve them." I paused briefly, allowing a look of disappointed sorrow to cross my brow. "My circumstances are so reduced, I have to part with them. Unfortunately, my business dealings have not gone well of late."

No compassionate look entered the widow's visage. If anything, a look of steely determination now took over her countenance. "I am prepared to double the value of any competing offer."

Trying to conceal my joy at having sprung the trap so dexterously, I agreed to produce the documents as soon as I returned from France. She asked me no questions as to the exact whereabouts of these papers. Wisely, I volunteered no further information. And so I took my leave of her that day.

For the next two weeks, I was confined to my rooms in Battersea as I penned this set of Byron's letters to his beloved, my mother. Letters filled with undying love are difficult to write at any time, but especially so at the age of twenty, by which time one knows full well that all romantic expectations are a grand illusion. Nevertheless, I soldiered on with this arduous task and, on the agreed day, I presented myself again at Mrs. Puddicombe's.

When she entered her sitting room, she looked utterly exhausted, observing that she was in the midst of a horrible bout of the vapours. She could not read the letters today, she vouchsafed. Three days at the earliest. I tried to conceal my disappointment, being especially needful of the yet unnegotiated sum. She was obviously in no frame of mind for a protracted conversation. Trying to make a virtue of necessity, I offered to return in two or three days. She seemed agreeable to this. As tactfully as I could, I introduced the question of price.

"Mr. Maggs has offered a thousand guineas."

This shook her from her lethargy. "As much as that? I am amazed. Two thousand guineas for such a small assortment?" She cast a woeful glance at the exceedingly thin pile of letters held together by a green silk ribbon. "I am a person of my word. You shall have your money. Return here in three days."

Having become slightly suspicious of my generous patron, I asked if a messenger could collect that sum on

my behalf. She nodded: "It makes no difference to me."
Perfunctorily, she waved her hand in dismissal. As I left
the room, she wiped her troubled brow with a large
cambric handkerchief.

My suspicion of the widow had been aroused by what
seemed an attempt on her part to conceal anger towards me
while she maintained a bout of melancholia had invaded
her. Two days after this interview, I ventured into Soho to
inspect the various vagrants who filled the streets. There
were not many to choose from. Poverty had stamped
virtually each face with ruthless cunning. I was about to
give up, having resolved to attend at Chiswick in person.

Then, I noticed a small and exceedingly thin young
man clothed, as all these persons were, in rags. What
attracted my attention was his smile. Despite the dirt
engrained into every pore of his miserable being, he had a
general air of benignity. I decided to approach him.

"Sir, do you inhabit the streets or do you have a roof to
call your own?"

Used to this kind of interrogation, he bowed slightly.
"The open air has long been my home."

"Do you have any manner of occupation?"

"Well, I did once, but that has vanished."

"Are you a rascal or a person with some claim to
honesty?"

"Honesty has always been my companion. I have never
abandoned him."

That did not seem a counterfeit reply. I asked his name,
which was Theo.

"Theo, could you act for me in a small matter? I have an
appointment in Chiswick tomorrow, but another, even
more pressing engagement has presented itself. I need
someone to collect a small parcel and return it directly to
me here." He nodded assent. "I take it you have no other
clothing?," I inquired. He said that was so. So, I agreed to
pay him five pounds for his services on the following day
and purchased a presentable outfit for him from an
emporium specializing in attire for such rabble. That set me

175

back a pound. To my investment was added a further ten shillings to rent a suitable conveyance to transport Theo to Chiswick and back.

This train of events seemed to go smoothly on the appointed day. The chaise was ready, and Theo's outfit made him look barely presentable. I sprinkled some rosewater on him before he set out, hoping this substance would cover up his stench for two or three hours. The driver and Theo were to meet me four hours later at exactly the same location. I must admit that the time passed slowly, although I decided to alter my appearance slightly. I removed my hat, allowing my long hair to fall free; I also removed my topcoat. Not exactly a disguise, just a slight rearrangement.

At the appointed time, the carriage made its way to the agreed-upon rendezvous. From a block away, I espied the driver — seated next to an unknown man — searching up and down the street, presumably for me. I stayed put. The carriage wandered away several times before settling once again in the same spot. I waited a further half-hour, at which point another male person — not Theo — emerged from the carriage. Quickly, I made my way to my lodgings. No one was there to waylay me. George Gordon DeLuna Byron vanished from the face of the earth.

Four days later, I learned Theo had been apprehended as soon as he arrived at Chiswick, accused of having stolen documents in the good lady's possession, for which he was demanding ransom. He was conveyed to Newgate and, after a brief stay there, transported to Australia.

From what I subsequently gathered, the widow had her own way of sniffing out forgers. She did not really know the letters were faked, but a strange conviction had overtaken her. Although she had never met him in the flesh, she was convinced she would have been Byron's ideal partner and helpmeet. Such feelings made her enormously jealous of the "real" women in Byron's brief life. In fact, she hated them. A man such as myself was anathema to her because I was the physical evidence of such an attachment. The ripe sexuality of the letters I penned was a further affront

176

because too much adoration — an excess of intimacy — infused them. Byron could never have felt that way for the Countess DeLuna and so, to her mind, the letters had to be counterfeit. A strange method to unmask a forger.

One of the most unexpected benefits of my huge crop of Byron letters (a grand total of 232 over a period of fifteen years) was the huge advance I garnered in 1875 from a London publishing house — to whom I was known as Griffin Warman — that commissioned me to write a life of Byron based on the plethora of new letters which had been unearthed.* What goes around can come around in the most unexpected ways.

Such was the case of my dear friend, Charles Raleigh, a direct but penniless descendant of Sir Walter. He became a forger, he claimed, in the same way a woman becomes a whore. "First, I did it to please myself, then I did it to please my friends, and finally I did it for money." He was an artist of the first magnitude, the author of the most beautiful letters of Dryden and Pope.

Charles spent his spare moments at the Public Record Office, laboriously copying out all the documents which demonstrated his Raleigh connection. Frequently, he showed me these transcriptions, proving his rightful identity. The sad truth was that it became evident after he died that he was born, Francis Simpson, the son of an itinerant labourer. Did he know his true identity or did he manufacture a lineage in order to prove his own worth to himself?

The course of my own life is best seen as a demented form of hopscotch. Always trying to find my way through the various steps of my chosen profession, I always had to hold one foot in the air; fearful of losing my balance, I had

---

*EDITOR'S NOTE: I gather this biography never appeared, but a distinguished Byron scholar, a colleague of Stephen's, has informed me that the most recent *authoritative* edition of the poet's letters accepts all the forged missives as genuine. Thus, all life histories of the poet-adventurer must be considered fictions.

to stay within the lines lest I should crash. Like my parents, I was not heathen in the carnal parts. I would form an attachment, break it, move on to another one, and so forth. The focus of my existence was the wonderful documents I wrote in the guise of others. As the century came to a conclusion and some early hints of modernism could be discerned, I took my own life by drinking a massive quantity of laudanum. I died on 31 December 1899.

part eight

Tom

I

Now that Eliza and Helen have made you aware of the "truth" behind the so-called Wainewright murders, I am of two minds. I am glad to have been let off the hook. Now you know that I was — for the most part — an innocent bystander drawn into the machinations of an evil woman.* On the other hand, the truth has not really freed me from the past. Would I have ever made it into, say *Chambers*, if the poisonings had not been attributed to me? Would my various bits of writing have been good enough to get me any kind of entry there? Would Dickens, for example, have shown the slightest interest in me if I was not a malefactor?

Although Wilde made some unpleasant observations about me, he remains my greatest

---

*EDITOR'S NOTE: I must confess that I was at two or three junctures reduced to tears when receiving Tom's final transmission, wherein my protagonist encounters further obstacles and nobly grapples with them. For me, his life history testifies to the nobility of the human spirit, its refusal to bow to indignities and injustices.

defender. A person who suffered tremendous setbacks in his own life, he was generous in asserting I had a sincere love of art and nature. Moreover, he wisely observed, "there is no essential incongruity between crime and culture. We cannot rewrite the whole of history for the purpose of gratifying our moral sense of what should be." Where there is no moral sense, there need not be any guilt.

Since I served as an inspiration for fiction, the mere facts of my physical existence are of absolutely no consequence. Yet, like most people, I crave notoriety, but I also want it to be bestowed upon me for the right reasons. Like unconditional love. But now I have the uneasy feeling that revised editions of all those biographical dictionaries may decide to exclude me. What if — an even more horrible thought — Eliza replaces me in those books? I am now on the horns of a whole new dilemma.

The politics of fame are exceedingly tedious. Perhaps I can offer you further evidence of my essential worthiness by telling you of my subsequent life as a runaway, of my existence as a serial killer, who, in fact, never harmed anyone of consequence? Yet, I remain deeply worried: is there anything about the essential me which can still make me a celebrity? If I am a fake poisoner and, by definition, a fake criminal, is there anything left? Who cares if I forged papers which simply released my own money to me?

Although she would never acknowledge it, Eliza bungled Helen's murder. Madeleine had obviously lost confidence in her half-sister's ability to pull off a successful chicanery against the insurance company. That is why she killed herself: she had imagined a style of life to which she had never before aspired. Her poverty-stricken imagination had been fired up. Once enlivened, her fancy escaped its Pandora's box. Then, she became frightened that the ploy would not work. She could not go on.

I didn't break Madeleine's heart — I suspect there was not much of a heart to break. And I don't think she cared that much for that old faultfinder, Helen. Madeleine had a crisis in confidence. After her death, I tried to soldier on, but I became more and more certain that the insurance companies were conspiring against me — and more and more frightened that the identity of the surviving sister — now an heiress — would be uncovered.

Understandably, then, I was badly discouraged after Helen's death. It was a tight, uncomfortable existence on Conduit Street. No longer did any of the neighbourhood's many amusements — the galleries of the Royal Society of Painters in Water Colours, Atkinson the Perfumer, outside which a bear was chained (his grease, perfumed with attar of rose, was the pomatum used by the Regent), the dazzling displays in Collingwood's jewellery shop — hold any charm for me.

For a variety of reasons, everyone's nerves were frayed. So in May 1831 I left for France, where I led a quiet, sedentary life. I resided briefly in Boulogne and Paris, wandered around Brittany, and then settled at St. Omer the following year. There, I received a visit from a law clerk appropriately endowed by the surname Young. He was employed by Acheson, my lawyer. I willingly signed the documents which this young man presented for my signature and even put him up for a few nights. In return, this impudent person, upon his return to London, advised everyone that I was living in a lonely country house with a wealthy old Frenchman. Without levelling any specific charge against me, he stated: "I did not like the look of things."

I lived a quiet life in France, acted as secretary to Monsieur J_____ and received money from time to time from my old chum, Barry Cornwall, who made sure that history was well aware of his generosity: "At the time [1833] I received a letter from him asking for a very small loan or gift in money, which I of course sent to him. The letter was in his usual fantastic style. But when he had to tell of his wretched state, his tone deepened. 'Sir, I starve,' he said, adding that he had been obliged to pawn his only shirt, in order to enable him to pay the postage on the letter. His letter exhibited great depression."

I suppose that a person accused of being a serial killer must be prepared for the hysteria that will follow him and for the unpleasant fact that all the unsolved murders that occur within a 100-mile radius of his subsequent places of residence will — on little evidence — be attributed to him. This was the real cause of my second "great depression." Here is a tiny catalogue of the scurrilities directed against me:

LEGEND ONE. During 1829–30, I became the close friend of a gentleman and his daughter from Norfolk, who, when they subsequently took up residence in Boulogne, I visited. I inveigled this estimable person to taking out a life insurance policy (to which I was not the beneficiary) in order to poison him so that the insurer would have to pay out £3000. One evening when coffee was brought in after dinner I squeezed poison from one of my numerous rings into the cup of this friend, who died shortly afterwards of convulsions. Wilde provided his own idiosyncratic "reading" of this supposed event: "His aim was simply to revenge himself on the first office that had refused to pay him the price of his sin."

LEGEND TWO. The police found discrepancies between my account of my reasons for visiting France and the ostensible facts. Those authorities, in subjecting me to their customary xenophobia, found that I carried about with me some of the powder of the *nux vomica*, otherwise known as strychnine, which was used in many places in that country for poisoning vermin, dogs and cats, and even rabbits. With a Gallic shrug, they put it all down to Monsieur Anglais's country of origin.

LEGEND THREE. I absconded to France in 1831, and resided for some time at Calais and also at Paris. In the former place I became personally intimate with a married female, whom fear of detection or some other strong motive induced me to poison. Not only was this female extremely fond of me, but her sister also became attached to me, and subsequently followed me to England, when I returned there. You will note that this piece of gossip has as its basis in fact a distorted retelling of my involvement with the Abercromby sisters.

The preceding apocrypha ascribe two more murders to me and suggest that I always carried poison on my person (presumably in a Borgia-style ring). What is true is that I had decided not to return to England, a resolve which was strengthened when in January 1835 the extraordinarily efficient Bank of England discovered that I had many years before imitated the signatures of my uncle and two cousins. A warrant for my arrest was issued, and the bounty-hunters, the brothers John and Daniel Forrester, paid me a friendly visit. According to the *Times*, they were unable "to accomplish anything except the object of seeing him." When they asked when I was likely to set foot in England again, I told them that I was unable to provide them with any particulars.

As you can imagine, 1835 was a particularly disastrous year for me. After the Bank of England's "discovery" that they were victims of a fraud, my suit *Wainewright v. Bland and Others* was heard in the Court of Exchequer by a special jury before Mr. Justice Abinger. The austere Sir William Follett — engaged by Eliza — headed the team which appeared on my behalf, whereas the obnoxious Attorney-General (Sir John Campbell) — a master of paralogical argument — led the opposing forces representing Imperial Insurance.

Before pointing out that Dr. Locock's post-mortem had revealed no evidence of foul play, my attorneys observed that I was only the nominal plaintiff since Madeleine Abercromby (now Mrs. Wheatley) was the beneficiary of her sister's estate. Then the actuary from the Imperial asserted that Helen had attempted to deceive him when he questioned her about seeking coverage from a wide variety of firms.

Sarah Handcocks was called by the Attorney-General to testify that, unlike my uncle George, I had sometimes been tardy in paying her wages. "Tom still owes me two or three pounds," she proclaimed. Harriet Grattan mentioned how she had seen Madeleine administering a jelly powder to her half-sister at twelve o'clock on the day of the latter's death. Mrs. Nicoll, my landlady in Conduit Street, then testified that Helen had been a "blooming" girl.

Dr. Locock offered evidence as to how generous and kind Eliza and I had been to his poor patient. Under cross-examination, he admitted that he had not used a lens to examine the contents of her stomach; however, he had noticed a few little specks under the coat of it, but whether extravasated or not he could not say. The Attorney-General attempted to shake the witness, even though Locock stuck to his story that there was no real evidence of foul play.

Further insinuations were introduced by the Attorney-General when he called Thomas Graham, a surgeon residing at Turnham Green, who had long been our family doctor at Linden House, as a witness. He testified that, at my request, he had examined Helen in 1830 and found her an excellent "risk" for insurance. When she died so suddenly and mysteriously, he had written to me to ask that a post-mortem be undertaken. In my reply, I brushed him off by observing that Locock had already done one. Not satisfied, Graham had applied directly to Locock, who placed the contents of the stomach in a bottle and then sent it to him. His observation: inflammation in one or two places.

Additional evidence by the Attorney-General centred on Helen's strange request for life insurance; he then spoke of Eliza's mysterious conduct. His defence was a tissue of insinuations, since he had no evidence to support murder. Not surprisingly, the judge, in his summation, claimed that "many of the circumstances of the poor young woman's passing were calculated to excite suspicion." On the other hand, if Miss A had effected the policy "for her own advantage" they would have to find on behalf of the plaintiff. This jury, now thoroughly confused, retired for two hours. In the end, they were six and six with no prospect for agreement.

The case was retried in December. My lawyers attempted to strengthen their case by calling Edward Hanks, the pharmacist who had attended Madeleine; at first, he proved a strong, unwavering witness: "I was called in to see her. I found her, to all appearance, labouring under a hysterical fit. I administered some medicines and went away. In the course of an hour I was sent for a second time, and saw nothing in the coats of the stomach to lead to a suspicion of foul play." Under cross-examination he was steadfast: "From what I had heard I should have thought the brain was affected from the continued fever. In my opinion the disease originated in the stomach. In fact, I consider the stomach began the disease. A strange condition actuated by coming in from the cold and immediately eating oysters."

Despite this major setback, the Attorney-General was exceedingly careful. He decided to leave the medical evidence alone and to put all his eggs into one basket: the multiple applications to insurance companies by a seemingly healthy young woman who had virtually no money. Why would she have tied money up in this way? He implied that Eliza and I had provided the funds in the expectation of a huge return on our investment. He insinuated that the young woman had agreed to this scheme because she was to be spirited away from England and would then die, say, by falling from a cliff. He offered his own flimsy — but accurate — theory: perhaps she had been assured that a corpse would at the appropriate time be purchased, placed *in situ*, and then be identified by Tom and Eliza as the dead girl.

This time through, the Attorney-General's ploy worked brilliantly. Although Abinger told the jury that they were not involved in a murder case, his summation was predicated on his sympathy for the plight of the insurance company and, after a few minutes' deliberation, the jury found in their favour. "On what grounds, gentlemen," asked

Abinger, "do you find your verdict?" "We find on two
grounds, believing that there was concealment by Miss
Abercromby and an evasion of the statute." Of course, they
firmly believed that I had poisoned my sister-in-law. My
reputation, already in ruins, was blasted. I was — in the
public eye — a murderer.

Your next question is an excellent one: why return to
England, having been branded *in absentia* a murderer? My
decision has exercised many imaginations — and allows me
the pleasure (and indulgence) of compiling two further lists,
the last ones to which I shall subject you. Here are four
explanations of my surprising behaviour:

A: "I have heard it whispered that a lady was involved —
not Mrs. Wainewright; for the husband and wife separated
in 1831, to meet no more."

B: "Some strange mad fascination brought him back. He
followed a woman whom he loved. He knew that his forgery
had been discovered and that by returning to England he
was imperilling his life. Yet he returned. Should one
wonder? It was said that the woman was very beautiful."

C: Very inventive story of how one of the actuaries had
fallen in love with Helen and decided to revenge her death.
This mysterious person "even followed the villain
Wainewright to Boulogne, and back again to England
where, as soon as he arrived, his pursuer set Forrester, the
police officer, upon him."

D: "It is quite probable that the brothers Forrester,
observing on their visit to Wainewright in 1835 his
disinclination from the English scene, had employed a
fascinating decoy to conjure him across the channel.
Unhappily, the police archives preserve no dossier or
records of the case."

My motive is open to question. This is as it should be, but even the accounts of my arrest differ widely:

1. "He now took up his quarters at an hotel in Covent Garden. When he went into a sitting-room in the basement to draw down the blinds, a noise in the street attracted his attention, and he pushed aside the blind for a moment to see what it was. Someone outside was heard to exclaim, 'That's Wainewright, the bank forger.' Bow Street and Covent Garden are neighbours; the speaker was Forrester, the runner, who had seen the runaway in France, and instantly recognized him. He was arrested, charged, and locked up." Curiosity killed this cat.

   NB: Wilde accepted this version but, as was his wont, imposed his own point of view on the situation: "A noise in the street attracted his attention, and, *in his artistic interest in modern life*, he pushed aside the blind for a moment."

2: "He was talking to a female, near a lamp, in Howland Street, Fitzroy Square, when he was seen by a policeman, who knew his person, and captured him. 'Mr. Wainewright,' the policeman said, 'I have been looking after you for a considerable time.' The forgery of which he had been guilty brought him to trial."

Although I offer my sincere apologies for the Snakes and Ladders approach to autobiography, I wish it were all as simple as historians and biographers have rendered it. I had not fallen in love. In April 1837, after all my efforts at obtaining a fair deal at law had failed, Edward Young suddenly reappeared at my doorstep. He had news of a distressing turn. My son, Griffiths, had contracted some horrid malady. He did not have long to live. Was there any way for him to see me again? Those are the circumstances under which I returned to England in May 1837.

In the last letter I received from him before I set sail for England, Mr. Young suggested — knowing I must take care to evade the police — that I meet a friend of his, Mrs. O'Neill, on Howland Street, Fitzroy Square, at eight o'clock on the evening of 9 June. I should simply walk the street — the lady would make the first move. Only when the coast was completely clear would she approach me. She would then conduct me to Griffiths.

Despite the danger, I was filled with joy at having returned to London. In order to outwit the police, I had grown a beard and moustache. Nevertheless, I was not deeply apprehensive that evening. Suddenly, a heavily veiled woman made her way up to me. She stood before me, studying my face intently. Then she dropped the veil. It was Mrs. Wheatley.

"Are you so surprised to see me, Tom?"

"Zounds, I am! You are like a ghost!"

"If your machinations had worked, I would be a ghost." Her countenance, as usual, was harsh and accusing. Then she smiled. "I must inform you of your situation. Although the Lord said 'Revenge is mine,' I have decided to take it into my own hands. Mr. Young is in my employ. I sent him to France in order to entice you back here. The Forrester brothers — the bounty hunters — have been informed of your whereabouts this evening and will be here shortly to apprehend you. I imagine that you will be charged with forgery and will be punished accordingly." She took a long pause. "If you divulge my new identity, things will go even more badly for you since your role in a series of murders will be divulged. Lizzie and Griffiths will also fall with you. I advise you to keep your mouth shut."

At that very moment, Daniel Forrester ran up to me and tapped me sharply on the arm: "Ah, Mr. Wainewright, how do you do? Who would have thought of seeing you here?" By this time, my sister-in-law had disappeared, and Forrester was in the process of removing the only weapon on my person: a small dirk in a sheath.

Of course, I had no way of knowing that Mr. Young was

a decoy in the service of Mrs. Wheatley. I should also like to remind you that Mrs. Wheatley in her account has not "shared" the above information with you: how trustworthy is the most seemingly reliable of the witnesses who have appeared before you?

The reports in the *Times, Morning Herald, Morning Advertiser,* and *Morning Post* about my conversation with the presiding magistrate, Sir Peter Laurie, are substantially accurate:

SIR PETER: "Do you wish to ask any questions?"

THE PRISONER: "None at all at present. I am not yet steady in my head. I was arrested but yesterday, and have not had time to communicate with my friends."

SIR PETER: "The charge is a serious one; do you wish for time?"

THE PRISONER: "I shall have to send to France for documents and wish to be remanded."

SIR PETER: "You shall be remanded till the latter end of next week."

The newspaper accounts are interesting on several scores. I have become the "Prisoner" whereas the Magistrate has retained his name. What does this say about the presumption of innocence? Second, Laurie says the charge was a "serious" one: how serious is a case of forgery wherein a person liberates his own money? I did not steal from anyone; I was simply making my own inheritance available to myself at a convenient time. In the mid-nineteenth century, forgery was still a crime for which one was routinely executed. So there was the distinct possibility that I could be slaughtered for prematurely gaining access to the funds left to me by my grandfather.

In 1822, in one of my little prose pieces, I had imagined my hero imprisoned for theft: *"Van Vinkbooms* week-long sickness and subsequent death. So Locock must bear part of the responsibility for her death. His initial unwillingness in his post-mortem examination to discern any evidence of foul play may have been a cover-up: he may have feared that Madeleine's death occurred as a result of his incompetence. Remember, his medical authority had been called into question by the presence of the apothecary.

Let bygones be bygones. As you can appreciate, I have always been a realist, and, as soon as Madeleine felt compelled to eat the oysters, I knew that my best-laid plan was doomed to failure. When I wanted to, I couldn't save someone from death. But I could force Helen into compliance. Unlike Tom, the incurable optimist, I was certain that the insurance companies would never pay up. In her turn, Helen proved to be a proficient blackmailer, so I had no choice but to allow her departure with Mr. Wheatley.

Lambeth was not the most illustrious of neighbourhoods for a woman with aspirations. The two rooms to which Griffiths and I migrated and were now confined were in an even more dilapidated state than anything we had experienced in Conduit Street or Pimlico. Literally, I had to live a hand to mouth existence — and, at the risk of mixing too many metaphors — from pillar to post. Mrs. A's property had been sold off long ago. I had a few, "authentic" pieces left which I gradually disposed of through Christie's. I put the touch on the Fosses, Tom's cousins, and, in this way, could exact gifts of ten or twenty pounds on an irregular basis. I attended the proceedings in Chancery only once (the day Helen espied me). Otherwise, that part of my life was over.

Obviously, I had to make a living. As a young girl, I had endured the rudimentary training in water colouring, one of the requisites in my century for a "well-educated" woman of genteel background. During the years I lived with Tom, he encouraged me to pursue this interest and introduced me to some of the basics in the use of oil and crayon. My husband, who was a more than adequate teacher as well as being an excellent draughtsman, imparted excellent skills to me. Having educated me in the basics, he taught me, as you *now lies in Horsemonger Gaol under sentence of death for a robbery in the British Museum.*" Art and reality had now come into grisly conjunction.

No one ensconced in Newgate could keep his right mind for long. The pretentious exterior of the building was filled with the statues of exemplary figures, including one of Dick Whittington and his cat. That particular touch was far-fetched, almost as if man and cat were proclaiming their moral virtue at the expense of the inmates. I suppose the designer of the building was saying that there were forms of cunning other than those practised by the criminal kind. Of course, so much money having been spent on the sumptuous facade, the misery of the interior was aggravated. Newly arrived prisoners were beaten and bullied by the inmates; the keeper and his turnkeys sold a wide variety of articles: candles, spirits, bread, and water — these essentials were not provided gratis; for example, private rooms — like mine — were only available if one were willing to pay an enormous consideration. The sickly smell of disease invaded the entire place; Newgate Market, devoted to meat, provided an additional stench.

Not only did I have to worry about losing my life, I had become a celebrity and had to put up with a series of visitations by persons doing research on the criminal mind. On 27 June, Dickens and some of his associates made a circuit of nearly all the London prisons; at Newgate they came upon me. One of them shouted: "My God! there's Wainewright!" They seemed startled by my shabby appearance, greasy, discoloured hair, and dirty moustache. (From this encounter, Dickens reinvented me as the sinister Vernon Slinkton in his short narrative, *Hunted Down*, a real piece of hack work. I curse him for that — I am worthy of far finer prose from that distinguished pen.) One of my visitors that day left this account: "He turned quickly round with a defiant stare at our entrance, looking at once mean and fierce, and quite capable of the cowardly murders he had committed."

I'm not sure I looked "mean" or "fierce," perhaps a bit defiant. After all, I had been reduced to the status of a performing bear and was deeply resentful. As usual, Oscar Wilde has taken considerable liberties in his role as biographer. Having heard of my encounter with Dickens, he fashioned the following statement: "Others had more curiosity and his cell was for some time a kind of fashionable lounge. Many men of letters went down to visit their old literary comrade."

Insurance agents and would-be hacks are not, by my definition, men of letters. However, one wag provided a "transcript" of a conversation he "overheard" between myself and an officer from the Imperial:

"I do not intend to preach to you — that would be idle; but I ask you, as a man of sense, Mr. Wainewright, whether you do not think your courses of action have been, to say the least, very absurd?"

"No," I rejoined, "no. I played for a fortune and I lost. They pay me great respect here, I assure you. They think I am here for £10,000, and that always creates respect."

"Well, but," said the investigative reporter, "if you look back upon your life, and see to what it has brought you, does it not demonstrate to you the folly of your proceedings?"

"Not a bit," I replied. "I have always been a gentleman, always lived like a gentleman, and I am a gentleman still. Yes, sir, even in Newgate I am a gentleman. The prison regulations are that we should each in turn sweep the yard. There are a baker and a sweep here besides myself. They sweep the yard; but, sir, they have never offered me the broom."

Most of the other accounts of my time at Newgate are fictional or badly distorted, such as the infamous exchange between myself and Hotten the publisher.

"Why did you poison your sister-in-law?"

"Why, I don't know, except that she had such thick ankles."

I was looking for a witty reply. Accused of being the aesthete-poisoner, I attempted to live up to the reputation. You will note that I actually cited Madeleine's observation about Helen, which Eliza had repeated to me. If you are accused of a crime, there is a tendency on the part of the accused — no matter how innocent he may be — to live up to that reputation.

At this time, I was fortunate — and desperate — enough to be able to secure my life by entering into an elaborate arrangement with the Bank of England and the insurance companies. In December 1836, Mrs. Wheatley — prodded by Eliza — had entered yet another action for the recovery of the insurance money payable on Helen's death. Now that I had been apprehended, the insurance companies were in grave danger of having to pay up: if Mrs. Wheatley had done nothing to effect her sister's death and was the legitimate heir of her sister, she was due to receive full payment on all the policies. My capture abetted her cause, since public sentiment was against me. So the insurance companies approached the Bank: would the Bank be willing to allow me to plead guilty to the lesser charge of uttering a forged document (not a capital offence whereas forgery was) in consideration of the companies assisting the Bank in the future?

The Bank was delighted to go along with this: they really didn't want even a notorious murderer to be hanged for the crime of stealing his own money. I then provided the insurance companies with a memorandum in which I named my wife as the chief conspirator and acknowledged my own small role in "Helen's" death. The insurance companies were delighted — and I thus blocked Eliza and Helen from receiving any money.

My troubles had only begun. Instead of receiving, as I was led to hope, a reprieve or a light sentence, I was transported for life to Tasmania. Mercy — as well as justice — is blind, despite what Portia rather naively proclaimed. I put the matter well towards the end of my life when I lamented: "*I was forthwith hurried, stunned with such ruthless perfidy, to the hulks at Portsmouth, and then in five days aboard the* Susan, *sentenced to a Life in a land (to me) a moral sepulchre.*" Before going on the *Susan*, I penned a letter to

Barry Cornwall, which reads in part: *"They think me a desperado. Me! the companion of poets, philosophers, artists, and musicians, a desperado! You will smile at this — no, I think you will feel for the man, educated and reared as a gentleman, now the mate of vulgar ruffians and country bumpkins!"*

II

I had heard — especially at Newgate — of the hulks at Portsmouth, Deptford, and Woolwich, places rife with filth and disease, especially the dreaded typhus. These vessels were huge old warships now living out their last years as water prisons for convicts on the way to the antipodes. In effect, they were floating slums to which a variety of excrescences had been added: deckhouses, platforms, lean-tos, all manner of unseemly structures. Bedding was strung out to air between the stumps of the mast, the gunports barred with iron lattices. To some deluded, romantic souls they looked like oscillating Piranesi ruins. They did not appear in such a picturesque fashion to me as the longboat on which I was a passenger drew near to my new gaol.

High above my head, I saw the battered figurehead which was all that remained of the old man-of-war's former glory. As our boat slowly made its way to the gaping hole carved at the side of the huge leviathan-like vessel, my nose was overcome with the dank, ripe odour of urine and faeces. I thought of that sad line in Lamentations 4: "They that were brought up in scarlet embrace dunghills."

As soon as our party reached the opening, we were quickly and brutally shuffled into a small, caged room where our hair was clipped. We were soaked in a cold bath and arrayed in uniforms. Each piece of clothing in which we were originally attired had a knife thrust through it: it was now the property of the Queen. Then, we were attired in rags. When I inquired of the Quartermaster if I might retain my silk shirt, so chafed was my skin by the one he had given me, he threatened to flog me for impudence. Then, he informed me that in my case all my clothes would be burned. (I was not altogether surprised to see him sporting my hat, shirt, and scarf two days later.)

A fourteen-pound iron was attached to the ankle of every single captive, an impediment meant to deter anyone who might consider a swim to shore. Some prisoners were even more heavily ironed: they could not afford the requisite bribe or "easement" which would inspire a gaoler's mercy. On my hulk, there were almost five hundred souls, a large number of which were "Johnny Raws," blockheads who were more fools than villains. These men — who were without funds of any kind — were even more cruelly and barbarously treated than the other captives.

Since my stay in Portsmouth was to be of very short duration — less than a week — I was not compelled to work on a chain gang in the government dockyards. One fellow prisoner, a graduate of Cambridge, was deeply mortified when his eye looked one day into the face of a fellow student at Peterhouse. His only consolation was that his face was so smudged and cadaverous-looking that his former crony could not possibly have recognized him.

Tobacco was the most desired commodity in that horrible dungeon, but it was officially denied us. Thus, trafficking in the forbidden drug was the source of our guards' real income. Plainly it was no secret that the prisoners had access to it, since the stench of tobacco frequently surpassed that of urine, faeces, and decomposing food.

During my brief sojourn near the margin of the shore, accompanied by the relentless movement of the grey heaving water, I noticed a curious couple, two extremely strange-looking creatures. The younger of the two was clad only in black. He was of medium height, well-made, and possessed facial features of extreme, almost effeminate delicacy. Mr. Silverthorpe may not have been strange-looking, but he carried himself in a most peculiar manner, as if the slightest breeze, for instance, might waylay and thus destroy him. In order to counter any such dangerous intrusions, he moved in an almost feline way, his joined hands held out in front of him as if to detect any unfriendly force he might encounter. His deeply inset, green eyes seemed almost slanted, flickering wildly as he studied every situation quickly and decisively.

A creature who seemed as nervous as any cat I have ever encountered, he was extremely indecisive, frequently asking the older man, his servant, for his opinion in any new situation. "George," he once ordered his companion, "pray discover when we might best converse with the Quartermaster about our inadequate provisions. You must decide when he is to be approached. You must also make a list of what we require. I can no longer attend to such matters." Then, changing his tone entirely, he adjured him: "You must be certain I am looked after with due ceremony. I cannot attend to myself further. My mind is cloudy with apprehension and anxiety."

If the younger man, who must have been five and thirty, bore some resemblance to a would-be Hamlet, his companion-servant, who was not required to wear a leg iron, looked like an attendant lord, a Rosencrantz or Guildenstern. He was a giant, whose costume was a tunic made of thick cloth, once pale yellow in colour. A tunic belt split his long torso in two. His hair — of which he had an abundance on his pate and on his face — was a pure glistening white. When in the company of the young man, George was the model of decorum, attending quietly to his master's every wants. On the few occasions when I saw him by himself — say, on the hulk's deck — he carried himself as in a frenzy of despair, talking to himself in a berating tone of voice, castigating himself for numerous deficiencies.

I soon lost track of these two demented creatures during my final leave-taking of England. The *Susan* left Portsmouth on 29 July 1837 with a total of 294 prisoners aboard, including myself. In that bobbing gaol I was to spend the forty-third birthday of my miserable existence. I suppose I was fortunate to survive (twenty-five died) the crossing, but nothing in my previous life — even the few days in

Portsmouth — had readied me for the sorry existence I now had to endure — not that our crossing was in any way remarkable compared to the even sadder fates visited upon others. There was a terrible historical irony in effect. I, the epitome of the Regency rake, left England forever a month after Victoria's ascension to the throne. In more ways than one, there was no place for the likes of me in Victorian England. With my fall came the end of the most elegant interlude in British history.

Our discomforts were considered mild. The hulk had its share of vermin, but the rats occupying the *Susan* were the size of small dogs, and they were not bashful in the slightest in making their many presences known. In heavy seas, the water sluiced through the vessel, chilling us to the bone and leaving our bedding a sodden mess. Most of the mangy excuses for livestock were washed overboard, and the crockery was almost completely broken to pieces. Pitch dropped from the seams and burnt the flesh of many prisoners. Fortunately, I escaped that indignity to my person.

Two pints of water were served to each of us every day, a quart of the putrid, blood-warm liquid. The contractors who controlled the *Susan* managed to feed us properly, although the staple of our diet was brined beef, which bore the nickname of "salt horse," a clue as to its real origins.

During the crossing, I once again paid notice to the Hamlet-like creature and his manservant. Although our sailor-captives continually and truthfully assured us that our Captain maintained the very highest standards in the treatment of transported prisoners, Mr. Silverthorpe continually beseeched our captors for special consideration. I could not discern why he felt so entitled. Like every other criminal on the vessel, he claimed to be completely innocent of the crime for which he had been convicted. In any event, he was merely accused, I heard him telling one of the sailors, of having stolen a trunk from a fellow actor; his guilt was completely circumstantial since the missing trunk had never been recovered.

I could not but notice that his constitution weakened

quickly and considerably within two weeks of the commencement of our journey. He could no longer take even the shortest exercise on the bridge. He now complained continually of this to George, whom, he felt, frequently overstepped the boundaries between servant and master, such as the many times he insisted Mr. Silverthorpe take water or consume a piece of bread.

One day, the young man approached me tentatively. "You seem to be a person of refinement. Not a common thief. What are you accused of?"

I told him I was of good family and that through an unfortunate misunderstanding had been convicted of making available to myself funds which had been left to me by my grandfather.

"Yes, it is obvious you are a person of good breeding," he assured me. He then informed me that his Christian name was Mansfield. "Have you ever kept servants?" he then inquired.

I told him such had indeed been the case. I could not refrain from pointing out that he was incredibly fortunate that George, who obviously had committed no crime, had volunteered to accompany him to the far shores of Australia.

"I daresay you are correct, but he is an old man. Who would give him employment in England?"

Even my jaundiced sensibility was startled by such ingratitude, but I allowed it to pass. Seeing that I was a person of "refinement," he decided to make me apprised of the story of his life. His confession was long-winded, rambling, but it had more than a few moments worthy of reflection.

Mansfield Silverthorpe — a stage name — was the legitimate grandson of Lord Langley. His mother, the peer's only daughter, had run away to Gretna Green with a young apothecary, a Mr. Vickers. Quite soon after the ceremony, Mr. Vickers died in a riding accident. The young widow went back to Hampshire to live with her father, her mother having passed away a decade earlier. Lord Langley was an officious but doting father who soon

197

became reconciled to his daughter's rebellious behaviour; when she announced she was pregnant, he even looked forward to the arrival of an heir to his vast estates. Unfortunately, Mrs. Vickers died in childbirth, leaving behind little Daniel. The distressed parent became an angry grandparent, one who could not forgive little Daniel for having deprived him of his beautiful Susan.

As a boy, Daniel was looked after in material wants, but his spiritual needs received no attention. At the age of fifteen, the youth ran away from home, no longer wishing to be an encumbrance. He joined a troupe of players, obtaining employment as a general dogsbody. Gradually, he learned everything there was to be known about the theatre, discovering his destiny as an actor, one best suited to tragic parts. His talents were accorded to be of the first rank, but instead of praise he encountered the enmity of London's actor-managers because his talents outweighed theirs and those of their favourites. So, forever precluded from the limelight, his was a dim provincial existence.

His life and acting career went on in their desultory way until his final appearance as Hamlet. His Gertrude was a woman of remarkable beauty, a person he found abundantly attractive. His interest in her was returned, much to the envious anger of the actor playing the role of Claudius. Much bickering ensued, to the extent that Hamlet's quarrel with the faithless Gertrude took on an increasingly hostile edge, the violence of their emotional turbulence electrifying their audiences. Even more caustic were the exchanges between Hamlet and Claudius.

Then, suddenly, the actor playing Claudius disappeared. Curtain time arrived, and the performance had to be cancelled. A malicious rumour ensued that Daniel had been seen on the street quarrelling with his fellow actor. The town constable — they were in Derby — was alerted, and he questioned Daniel closely. Since he had no knowledge of the man's whereabouts, he proclaimed his innocence of any involvement. Subsequently, the company's Ophelia told the magistrate that she had seen Daniel with the actor's trunk, also missing. In fact, she had seen Daniel deliver the trunk to a gypsy peddler who had loaded the said trunk on to his cart. Although neither the driver nor his vehicle had ever been located, Daniel was tried for stealing the trunk, although the authorities were certain Claudius' corpse had been deposited therein.

There is a real limit — even under English law — as to how much circumstantial evidence can be entered into the courts of law. Daniel was tried and convicted of stealing the missing trunk, but, in essence, he was being punished for the crime of murder. For this offence, he was transported, despite the fact that his barrister pointed out to the judge and jury that the Ophelia had — as in the play — been spurned by her Hamlet, Mr. Silverthorpe.

This was a remarkable tale, rendered at times in the most affecting manner. Immediately, I could see how gifted a thespian my friend had been. During the next week, my new friend's state deteriorated rapidly. His condition, which was tubercular, left him both restless and exhausted. Daniel refused all ministrations of his caretaker, who nevertheless hovered near him day and night. Finally, my new friend passed away when we had been at sea for a month, his corpse unceremoniously thrown overboard.

George was devastated, lamenting in particular the fact he would have to book his return passage as soon as we arrived in Tasmania. I wished such an option was in my purview. The old man mumbled to himself even more than before, seemingly inconsolable for the loss of his master, it frequently being the lot of unimaginative members of the lower classes to harbour such sentiments for their betters.

Gradually, as if in sympathy to his young master, George's physical health deteriorated. By the time we were within a month of our destination, he took to his bed. One day, I asked if he would like me to convey his ration of water to him. "Please, sir," he responded. I fetched his water, poured it into his tumbler and then assisted him in drinking. Suddenly, he seemed to revive, thanked me for my kindness, and asked me to sit by his side.

"Daniel was very grateful to encounter a man of your station on our unfortunate voyage," he began.

I was a bit taken aback to hear George refer to his master in this way. Before, he had always referred to him as "Mr. Silverthorpe" in my presence. I think my astonishment must have betrayed itself in my expression, for he continued. "Daniel told you the story of his unhappy life, I believe?"

"He told me of his ancestry and his career on the stage; he even confided in me the circumstances of his transportation."

"Yes, yes," he nodded. Then he shook his head vigorously. "*None* of that is true."

I felt affronted. "Is that so, sir?," I inquired, allowing my scorn for his impudence full expression.

George's face darkened, tears forming. "Daniel was my son. I know the full circumstances of his sorry existence."

Seeing I was both astounded and agitated, he proceeded to tell me his version of the story of Daniel Vickers' life. The old man's name was Robert Vickers, at one time a prosperous farmer in Shropshire. He and his wife had the good fortune of having one child, whom they christened Daniel in honour of the brave Israelite who showed remarkable valour in the lion's den. As a child, Daniel demonstrated precociousness in language and all manner of verbal expression. At the village school, he was a wonder. As he grew older, he became rambunctious, informing his parents that his circumstances of birth had been concealed from him. He had to be the son of some great aristocrat, so keen were his powers of observation, so advanced beyond his supposed parents was he in his intellectual capacity. He became convinced he was the illegitimate offspring of some great lord. Husband and wife attempted to remedy the deficiencies in their son's understanding but to no avail. He remained obdurate in renouncing them.

Gradually, relations between parents and child worsened and, at the age of fifteen, the young man disappeared from home, taking with him over two hundred guineas worth of silver plate. Mrs. Vickers died some twelve years after her son abandoned home; she never set eyes on him again. After the death of his wife, Mr. Vickers sold his farm and all his worldly possessions and made his way to London, hoping to encounter his wayward offspring.

Once he reached the metropolis, the father did not have to search far to discover the son, who was a denizen of Gin Alley. When he was able to, Daniel worked as a "starglazer," one of those ruffians who cut the panes out of shopwindows and then help themselves to whatever is behind the glass. Such thieves sell the stolen goods, but, in addition, they also peddle the perfectly cut pieces of glass to householders. Mr. Vickers was appalled by his son's style of life but could do nothing to stop him.

In fact, so feeble had Daniel's mind become by the excessively heavy demands that the killer gin made on him that he considered himself to be a certain Mr. Mansfield Silverthorpe, late of the British provincial stage. His fantasy life became his real life. When Mr. Vickers attempted to apprise him of his identity as his father, the young man was flabbergasted, informing him that he was his "dresser," by the name of George. And so Robert Vickers, yeoman of the county of Shropshire, became a member of the theatrical profession.

For three long years, he ministered to his wayward child, until the son was apprehended when, in need of more drink, he agreed to assist a "till frisker" in emptying the contents of a till belonging to a grog merchant. He was apprehended, convicted, and sentenced to transportation. Mr. Vickers approached the authorities, who, shaking their heads in disbelief at such excessive parental concern, agreed to allow the grief-stricken father to accompany his son to the savage continent.

Mr. Vickers was pleased to have delivered himself of his remarkable tale, at such great variance with the one provided by his son. I thanked the father for his honesty, but I must confess I was badly shaken to hear Daniel had been a dastardly liar. The roots of art cannot reside in chicanery and madness. Of that primary truth, I desperately reassured myself.

I was not inordinately displeased when Mr. Vickers passed away a mere two weeks before we reached Tasmania.

III

On 21 November 1837, the ship anchored in the bay of Hobart, Van Diemen's Land. With Rome, Hobart shares the distinction of having been built on seven hills. There the resemblance ends. Small white houses dotted the huge harbour under the imposing shadow of Mount Wellington. Closer inspection revealed a shabby colonial town displaying the usual pretensions when colonials ape their homelands. From the *Susan*, I beheld the town as a pretty-enough confection; later that same day, I saw first-hand the rough, ready-made buildings of the place through a thick fog as my companions and myself were marched through it in chains to high-walled Hobart Gaol, the home of sixteen thousand prisoners.

A dog-in-the-manger attitude towards the French had first led the English to settle hot, humid, dank Van Diemen's Land (really, it should more appropriately have been called The Demon's Land) — a place that contained all the worst features inherent in the term "tropical" — in the early part of the century. The flooding of the Bass Straight twelve thousand years before had severed this sorry excuse for a eucalyptus forest from the island of Australia. So there it was, stuck on its own, the indigenous population being the Negritoes. Then, aboriginals were exported there; later, outlaw bushrangers.

Having seized the island, the English weren't sure what to do with it. Since the number of felons was increasing in Britain, which lacked the space to store them — and since they lacked imaginations — they decided to transform the island into a huge penal institution. The prisoners confined there were, as the ballad proclaims, "ranked up like horses" and chained to ploughs as beasts of burden. A fatal shore in every sense: disease abounding, cruelty unleashed, climate inhabitable. A place suitable only for wombats, wallabies, platypuses, and Tasmanian devils, those foul marsupial scavengers with their husky snarls and bad tempers.

When I first arrived in Hobart Town, I became Convict 2325. New arrivals such as myself were shown no clemency: they were "worked on the roads." Even though I pleaded with the Superintendent that I understood Latin and Greek, had been a prolific journalist, and was a first-rate artist, I was forced to undertake heavy manual labour. I am certain that this brutal treatment hastened the deterioration of my spine.

Life at the "Tench" was in every way degrading: we were chained up in separate cells; our uniforms were made of a smelly yellow cloth with the word "FELON" stamped all over it; we went to work in Indian file and were never allowed to speak to each other. The name "Tasmania" — not bestowed until the 1850s — was devised to have a touristy feel to it, reminiscent of such banalities as palm trees and cockatoos. There was nothing holiday-like in the conditions we faced, forced to mine the ungrateful soil for iron, zinc, and tin. Long days under a Mars-like sun.

After an initiation process which lasted three months, I became one of the prisoners who were designated "amenable." I was graduated from the road parties to the Lumber Yard, where the work also exacerbated the problems with my backbone. At that time, I was allowed to speak more freely with my captors, and, when I told them of my skills as an artist, I was invited to do portraits of them, their wives and children. Only because of my success in that endeavour was I transferred in February 1844 to the Colonial Hospital. The work was a bit lighter and was supposed to allow me time to paint. Theory did not follow practice.

203

The floors were never washed, days of excessive heat reduced the entire place to an inferno. The heavy smells of

urine and the foul stench from amputated limbs being burnt
were also not conducive to my best artistic endeavours. A
month after I began work at the Colonial, there was an
outbreak of typhoid. During those horrible days, I had the
pleasure in assisting Dr. Brodribb, a young man deeply
attuned to his patients. A cultivated soul, he had read
Hazlitt, De Quincey — even Tom Wainewright. When
Brodribb was transferred to the hospital on the land of the
Jewish Synagogue, I was heartbroken.

My abilities as an artist made me a person who was a
stranger to my fellow convicts and my would-be patrons. I
obviously did not inhabit either world. And so once again I
became the victim of misunderstanding, as can be seen in
this pen portrait of me by the appropriately named Dr.
Crooke:

> ... a man with a massive head, in which the animal
> propensities were largely developed, and with a
> great volume of brain. His eyes were deeply set in
> his head, he had a square solid jaw, wore his hair
> long, stooped somewhat, and had a snake-like
> expression, which was both repulsive and
> fascinating. His conversation and manner were
> winning in the extreme. He was not intemperate,
> but grossly sensual; with the intellect of a Pericles
> and the passions of a satyr. He used to take a dram
> of opium a day; and it was to procure this
> indulgence, that he practised painting. If
> commissioned to execute the portrait of a lady, he
> would always endeavour to give an erotic direction
> to the conversation; so that whatever admiration
> was felt for his genius, was neutralized by the fear
> and antipathy excited by his lewdness. The
> malignancy of his character seems to have been
> ingrained and ineradicable, and he took a perverse
> pleasure in traducing his benefactors. The only
> living creature for which he felt a sincere affection
> was a cat, to which he was much attached. Was

there a secret affinity between his own nature and that of his pet? Both could boast of the *patte de velours*, and both had a good deal of the tiger in their composition. He endeavoured to poison two people who had become obnoxious to him in Hobart Town; and no compunctious visitings of conscience ever interfered with the execution of any fell purpose upon which he had been resolved. One example of the savage malignity of his character will serve to show that we have not exaggerated its innate cruelty and depravity. While he was an inmate of the hospital, a patient entered against whom he entertained a grudge. Wainewright's educated and penetrating eye detected the presage of death in the poor fellow's face, and approaching him, he hissed into his ear with venomous earnestness: "You are a dead man. In four and twenty hours your soul will lie in hell, and my arm will be buried so deep," — touching his elbow — "dissecting it."

The only smattering of truth in Crooke's account concerns my revenge on the prisoner who tortured me. Any unseemly conduct towards a sitter would have easily brought my practice as a painter to an abrupt conclusion.

At the Colonial, serving with me, there was a slight wretch, perhaps five and thirty in years. Very similar in build and height to myself, the recently arrived rascal, who always looked rumpled, was inexplicably consumed with amiable spirits — especially to those in his charge. I learned something about medicine from Brodribb but much about nursing from Theo, who had worked at a number of jobs (had even served briefly as a porter at Christie's), eventually lost all employment, been rendered destitute, and lived on the streets of London until he was rather improbably convicted of trading in stolen letters. The charge against him was patently ludicrous: he was completely illiterate and would never have been able to read any document to

205

identify its contents. By my reckoning, his heart was too readily open, even though he correctly pointed out to me on more than one occasion that we were both innocent men charged with similar offences.

Even my jaundiced heart was moved by his kindness, although I could never grasp whence such cheerfulness derived. A strange, brave little man. Shortly afterwards, I became extremely light-headed one afternoon. I obtained permission to retire early that evening. During the night, I became suddenly and violently ill, my body wavering between extremes of cold and heat. As soon as my fever reached its pitch, it would break whereupon I would feel on the verge of turning to ice. My nose bled profusely, my appetite vanished, and my bowels gave out on me. For a day or two I was ambulatory, but, after that, I clung to my bed as my temperature rose steadily.

In my few moments of consciousness, I was frightened by the small, rose-coloured spots that spread over my torso — the hallmarks of typhoid. My body did not wish to labour on. A small, wiry man, I became a skeleton attached to a stomach constantly screeching in pain. I also became delusionary. Helen, Madeleine, my uncle George, Eliza, Griffiths, and even my grandfather haunted the nightmares that became my existence.

I was not a good patient. Between fits of consciousness usually occupied by vomiting, I was bad-tempered to Theo, who offered me words of encouragement.

"You will recover, Mr. Wainewright. You can be certain of that!"

"Don't offer me false assurances. I am too far gone for such pap."

"No false promises, Mr. Wainewright. You are strong enough to withstand the siege. Within a fortnight, you will be much improved. Like me, you have a strong constitution." He offered these observations while applying a cold compress to my forehead.

"You know nothing of my constitution. You are uniformly cheerful when there is absolutely no room for optimism."

"Oh Mr. Wainewright. You know many more things than I, but in this particular I am correct. The world we inhabit is all illusion. I am in touch with the wonders beyond the material world."

"Now, you speak nonsense. You know no such thing."

"Mr. Wainewright, sir, I do. From the heart." Suddenly, he became agitated, whilst pointing one of his tiny little hands in the direction of that organ. "I have no book knowledge; I know only the happiness that has always filled my spirit. I am not, as you suspect, a Quaker or some other sort of enthusiast. I know the truth of my own feelings."

I could not be but touched. At the very same time I thought him a simpleton. I was startled when he confessed to me one day that he had enjoyed — despite numerous setbacks — a happy existence.

"Pray sir, but how can that be so?"

"I have been content with what life has presented me."

"But it has bestowed nothing upon you."

"So it may appear, but I have many happy recollections from childhood. When, for instance, I was a small boy, I had the privilege of serving in a grand country house, wherein resided two young maidens of my own age. They were not twins, though close in age. I considered them angels." He paused, as if to consider the accuracy of what he was relating. He continued hesitantly. "Unfortunately, I was dismissed from my post and lost touch with those delightful creatures."

"So, in reality, life has been harsh?"

"Appearances are deceiving." He winked at me as a gesture of fellow-feeling and then offered the only remonstrance I ever heard cross his lips. "Sir, you give too much credence to the material world."

I kept my mouth shut. Perhaps, I wondered, the poor creature had some remnant of sense in him.

At the end of the third week after the onset of my illness, my bones still felt sore and useless, but I began to stay awake for longer periods of time. Soon after, my delirium vanished and my spirits were raised. I was still too ill to climb out of bed for more than five minutes at a time.

Theo remained unflagging in his attention but then he vanished. When I inquired after him, I was told he had become quickly and gravely ill. I am sorry to say Theo eventually succumbed to the dread disease that had nearly vanquished me. A week later when I arose briefly to relieve myself, I beheld his naked, bony corpse flowing down the stream near the hospital, his puny little arms cradling himself.

In contrast to that scoundrel Dr. Crooke, my artistic career in Tasmania has been romanticized in William Beatty's *Tasmania: Isle of Splendour*: "Quite a number of Tasmania's early society belles are the works of Wainewright. He caused many a flutter among feminine hearts, and society beauties used to beseech the gaol governor for permission to have their portraits painted by him. Their mothers or a chaperone would usually accompany them to Hobart Gaol while they 'sat' for their pictures. One can understand that the authorities and everyone else found it difficult to think of Wainewright as a murderer."

Mr. Beatty is gilding the lily. My life on Tasmania was hardly tinged with the glamour he bestowed on it. Were there really "society belles" or "beauties' in Van Diemen's Land? Isn't there some sort of inherent contradiction in yoking that place to any idea of refined living?

When anyone cross-questioned me about my past life in England and France, I whitewashed the truth a tiny bit but, despite my best efforts at reformation, the question of my reputation haunted me. In 1846, I became seriously ill again and became a patient in the hospital where I had once served as an orderly. My speech became slurred; I could not raise my head; I was incredibly lethargic. Sclerosis, melancholia, or both?

Earlier, in June 1843, my doctor friends had urged me to petition for my release. My petition of 18 April 1844 was not granted, but I was given a 3rd Class Probation Pass (3rd class prisoners were the most trustworthy). On 18 December 1845, I was at last granted a Ticket of Leave (restricted to Australia and New Zealand). So what did I do? I moved a stone's throw away to 8 Campbell Street, in the heart of Hobart's artistic district. Two eyewitnesses from that time have left accounts of me. One noted the peaked cap and long blue coat in which I was habitually clad; the other, a gilder and frame-maker, remembered me as "a tall foreign-looking man with dark complexion and moustaches. He chewed opium sticks and the saliva discoloured his mouth."

In November 1846, I suffered my first stroke and was admitted to St. Mary's Hospital. In my remaining ten months, I wanted to sort out the meaning of the various experiences I had endured. Thus, while passing time in death's ante-room, I looked back upon my youthful aspirations and realized that my true fame would have to rest on my work as a portrait painter in Tasmania. But there is a crushing, dreadful irony about those portraits. If you study them carefully, you will notice that the sitters are attired in the exact dresses and costumes in which they appeared before me. I was careful about such details, and I tried my very best to reproduce exactly the countenance of each. Once again, my truncated apprenticeship with Phillips proved invaluable.

Yet, the faces in the paintings always looked vastly different from the persons themselves. Most of the people who sat to me had coarse, large features, and yet all the surviving portraits are of faces which have a sweet, elfin quality. The sitters always liked the portraits, even though there was a remarkable discrepancy between what they looked like and what my pen and brush forced me to make them look like. I did not attempt to flatter, but I saw no truth in my extremely successful results. Was I trying to relive my lost youth or did I see into the deepest aspirations of my sitters and thus recreate their ideal selves? What force guided my hand and brush? The only portrait from Tasmania which is accurate is my self-portrait, dashed off at the request of one of my doctor friends. In that canvas, one sees a long, hideous face accompanied by small, receding eyes, rodent-like teeth, and unkempt, straggly hair; the sitter looks contemptuously at the viewer

In my last days, I tried to solve the riddle of all these portraits, but to no avail. I began to sleep for long stretches of time. I had a recurring dream of a small boy, one who had just learned to walk. His countenance was filled with joy, but I began to wonder if he was an evil sprite masquerading a mischievous intent. Whenever I asked his name, he would stop his promenade round my bed, curtsy, and — with the hint of a smile crossing his visage — wander out of my chamber. To this day, I have no idea of his identity.

On my final day, when I awoke, a woman was seated by my bedside. At first, I was certain that it was Mrs. Nuttall, the doctor's wife, but I had never seen her out walking in such finery. Her dress was of deep satin green, of a fashion common in the early days of the Regency. At first, I thought her face painted with white zinc, but then I noted that this might indeed be her natural complexion. The copious ringlets which flowed down her back were of the richest auburn. Then I observed that her eyes were emerald-coloured and that at the corner of each eye was an enormous tear, the size of a small pearl. As she whisked her head back and forth, the tears would vanish and then reappear.

"Do you not know me, Tom?"

"Madam, you have never sat to me, and I have never seen you on the street in Hobart Town."

"You knew me a long time ago."

"I do not recognize you."

A bit petulantly and condescendingly, the woman allowed a smirk to cross her face. "Dear Tom, of all the people you have ever known, you should recognize poor dear Madeleine."

The voice was indeed familiar. "Maddy, you have long been dead."

"Indeed so, Tom, and I have come to welcome you to my kingdom."

I found it impossible to think. I was very ill, my sensibility completely disorientated. I beheld everything —

the room, the woman — as if looking through thick white gauze. The woman certainly did not look like any memory I had retained of the dead girl. This woman carried herself with great assurance, with an almost matronly elegance. "You used to be so awkward, Maddy."

"Indeed, I was. You took advantage of me, Tom."

I could not but loose my temper. "You betrayed me! The scheme would have worked except for your rashness. We would have prevailed."

"Even I am amazed that you still see things in such a confined way. I was robbed of my life. Everything was snatched from me."

"You conspired with Lizzie and me. You were guilty of a crime. You lost your nerve."

"Is that really so, Tom? I fell in love with you. You were older than me. I had been tied to an awful mother and a dreadful half-sister. I did love Helen, but she was a charmless task-mistress who saw me as a mindless extension of herself. I needed to escape."

"So you joined our conspiracy."

"That was a great crime. I was tormented because I knew that Helen — despite her many faults — loved me. I pressed ahead. Then, I discovered that you had been unfaithful to me."

"Helen told me. She wanted me to come to my senses, be my old self. Of course, I was left with absolutely nothing. You did not really care for me; Lizzie was a cold-hearted wench. If Helen died, I would have no one, and I would be guilty of her murder. Finally, I took the recourse taken by women from time immemorial: I erased myself. And why not? I had nothing to lose."

"You make me sound so cold-hearted."

"But you were. During my final week of agony, you never visited with me. For her own ulterior reasons, Lizzie tried to save me; Helen was constantly at my side, although I could never ask her forgiveness because there was always someone else in the room."

She sucked her breath in. "You always allowed events

to unfold to suit yourself. That is a terrible crime. And you have never and will never understand the nature of your crime. And for that reason you will continue to pay a heavy price."

"I don't know what you mean. I have suffered enormously here."

"That is just a foretaste. Even after death, yours will be a restless spirit, one that will never find any peace. You will spend eternity attempting to justify yourself. Just as you are on the verge of self-vindication, the entire scheme will collapse because you will never be able to get ahold of anything more than a simulacrum of feelings. You will never even understand the agony that you yourself have endured. You had the experience but missed its meaning. For you, the examined life was not worth living. You are one of those unfortunate people who live for years without living at all." Having delivered herself of this tedious set of moral reflections, she vanished.

The daughters of Mrs. Abercromby were an exceedingly trite lot, women of excessively thick ankles *and* legs. As you can well understand, Maddy's little speech caused me to suffer the cerebral aneurism, of which I died on 17 August 1847.

ENVOI

Depleted though I may be by the task of transcription, I happily consign these voices to you, the reader.

If you are learned, you might consult the texts listed within my humble pages. Thomas Wainewright has preoccupied many writers. See for yourself how Dickens, Bulwer-Lytton, and Wilde, among others, rendered him into fiction. You may even consult Tom's critical essays, which are now being readied for publication by the Clarendon Press, Oxford. Or the new, scholarly biography, to be published at the beginning of the new millenium.

Modestly, I credit myself with the revival of interest in Tom Wainewright. I hope I have made a contribution to his reputation.

Like myself, you may find yourself gazing more critically at many of the canvases on display at art galleries. You may even wish to consult an expert about the authenticity of any Meissen figurines you own. Of one thing I am certain: you will be convinced of the integrity of the woman by the voices possessed.